Tales of the
Old North Shore

Tales of the
Old North Shore

Paintings and Companion Stories by Howard Sivertson

Lake Superior Port Cities Inc.
Duluth, Minnesota
1996

First edition published June 1996 by

 LAKE SUPERIOR PORT CITIES INC.
P.O. Box 16417
Duluth, Minnesota 55816-0417
USA
888-BIG LAKE (244-5253)

5 4 3 2

Sivertson, Howard, 1930-
    Tales of the old north shore : paintings and companion stories / by Howard Sivertson.
        p.   cm.
    Includes bibliographical references.
    ISBN 0-942235-29-0
    1. Superior, Lake – History – Anecdotes. 2. Superior, Lake, Region – History, Local – Anecdotes. 3. Superior, Lake, Region – Social life and customs – Anecdotes. 4. Superior, Lake, Region – Biography. 5. Superior, Lake in art. I. Title.
F552.S58 1996
977.4'9 – dc20   96-11970
                                                              CIP

Printed in the United States of America

    Editor: Paul L. Hayden
 Designer: Stacy L. Winter
   Printer: Davidson Printing Co., Duluth, Minnesota

This book is dedicated to
Chris and Annie

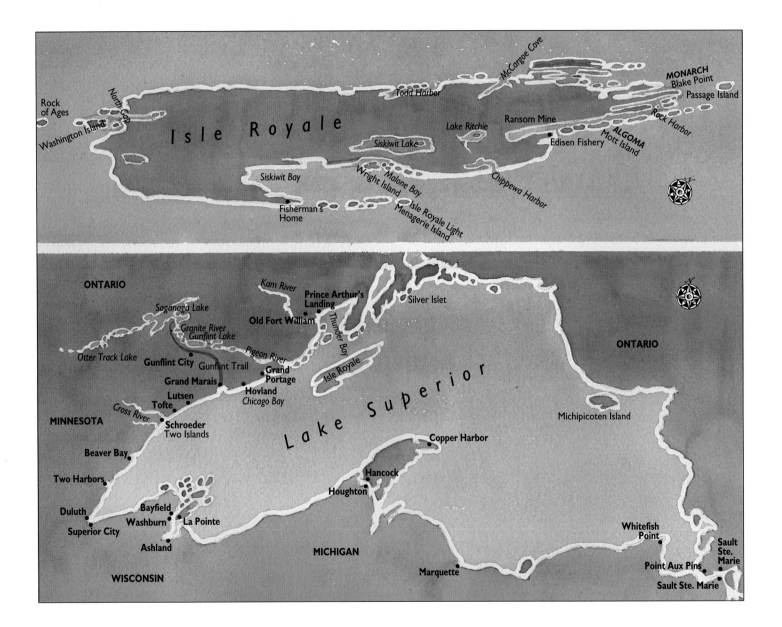

Isle Royale

Rock of Ages
North Cap
Washington Island
Todd Harbor
McCargoe Cove
MONARCH
Blake Point
Passage Island
Rock Harbor
Ransom Mine
ALGOMA
Mott Island
Lake Ritchie
Siskiwit Lake
Edisen Fishery
Siskiwit Bay
Malone Bay
Wright Island
Isle Royale Light
Menagerie Island
Chippewa Harbor
Fisherman's Home

Lake Superior

ONTARIO
Kam River
Prince Arthur's Landing
Silver Islet
Saganaga Lake
Old Fort William
Thunder Bay
Granite River
Gunflint Lake
Otter Track Lake
Gunflint City
Gunflint Trail
Pigeon River
Grand Portage
Isle Royale
ONTARIO
Grand Marais
Hovland
Chicago Bay
Lutsen
Tofte
Cross River
MINNESOTA
Schroeder
Two Islands
Michipicoten Island
Beaver Bay
Copper Harbor
Two Harbors
Hancock
Duluth
Bayfield
Houghton
Washburn
La Pointe
Superior City
Whitefish Point
Ashland
Sault Ste. Marie
MICHIGAN
Point Aux Pins
WISCONSIN
Marquette
Sault Ste. Marie

Table of Contents

Acknowledgments

Dr. Timothy Cochrane
Pete Edisen
Robert Hagman
Thom Holden
Ingeborg Holte
Milford Johnson
Justine Kerfoot
Patrick C. Labadie
Pat Maas
James R. Marshall
Walter Matthews
Roy Oberg
Peter Oikarinen
Dr. Willis H. Raff
J.C. Ryan
Arthur Sivertson
Stanley Sivertson
Brian Tofte

Cook County Historical Society
Grand Portage National Monument
Isle Royale Natural History Association
Isle Royale National Park Service
Lake County Historical Society
Lake Superior Magazine
Minnesota Historical Society
Old Fort William
St. Louis County Historical Society

And all patrons of my art
    who made this book possible

Preface

Howard Sivertson is a talented man. Not only can he create a memorable painting of the past, he does so with an attention to detail and historical fact that makes that painting more than an opinion. You can take it on faith that his research makes it a true representation of the time. Add to that his accompanying "tale," and you have a package that causes you to note the parallels reflecting from your own life.

Lake Superior's North Shore has challenged both explorers and inhabitants since the last glacier retreated some 11,000 years ago. The Sivertsons first saw the North Shore in 1892, and their first visit to Isle Royale in 1892 was quite an experience. The home they thought they would occupy was piled up in sections on the dock! Having come from Norway, where the limited livable land passed only to succeeding generations, this was quite a shock. It didn't take long for these new Americans to set fresh and deep roots on adjacent Washington Island, where the family still has ties.

Many of the most significant events are documented in Howard Sivertson's first book *Once Upon An Isle,* which reflects so much more than incredible paintings and lucid text. Most of these early families dealt daily with a simple challenge – survival. Few were comfortable with our English language to the point that they documented their activities. As success – and an occasional failure – blended into daily activities, happenings of the day were exchanged around the warmth of stoves in tiny homesteads.

The years rolled by and certain events gained the stature of timelessness. Be it the summer gatherings on the long beaches of Washington Harbor, or the ice-encrusted porches of extremely modest Duluth winter homes, they were repeated. Howard Sivertson's mother, "Myrt," could tell, in exquisite detail, everything about the sinking of the steamer *America.* Not remarkable, you might think, except that she told the tale in detail in 1965 – and the ship sank June 7, 1928! As a newlywed trying to establish her home on Isle Royale, her first guests were the stranded passengers of that ship.

And after he arrived in 1930, Howard, his formal name, was destined forever to be "Buddy" to the whole circle of his acquaintants, as well as his best friends. It has been a rare privilege to watch this fine artist combine firsthand experiences with an almost unmatched talent for bringing them to life using a canvas medium.

Always gifted, he labors to record and thus share his memories with an increasingly interested audience. As the many artistic talents of his daughter Jan became apparent, she opened a gallery in Grand Marais, Minnesota. Its success led to a second gallery in Duluth. Howard's work is exhibited in both.

Savor and meditate on the thoughtful gifts presented on these pages – it is Howard Sivertson's gift to you!

– James R. Marshall
Lake Superior Magazine

Introduction

It wasn't the best of times nor the worst of times. But it was probably one of the most interesting of times in the wilderness frontier surrounding Lake Superior. A good story requires an interesting, colorful and diverse cast of characters, and the Lake Superior region certainly had the characters during the pioneer years, from mid-1800s to the early 1900s.

The voyageurs were still paddling bark canoes between Canada's Fort William and Sault Ste. Marie, carrying Hudson's Bay Company officials and mail. Indians and half-breed ex-voyageurs began commercial fishing out of the abandoned stations of the American Fur Company. Mineral prospectors and miners swarmed the wilderness, hoping to strike it rich in gold, silver, copper and iron ore.

Sailing schooners and the first propeller ships were coming through the newly constructed locks at the Sault to form the lifelines to the roadless frontier. Many of them would become the victims of horrendous storms and hidden reefs of treacherous Lake Superior.

Colorful lumberjacks came to log the white pine used to build America's growing cities, while Scandinavian immigrants came to harvest Lake Superior's fish to feed the nation's families. Daring mailmen used small rowboats and dog teams to carry the mail throughout this vast roadless area to isolated settlements around the lake. The noble Indian was still independent and a major player on the pioneer stage.

On the lighter side are stories like the snoose-chewing moose who met the mail boat to beg passengers for tobacco. And the story about the commercial fisherman who loaded his cow in a skiff each day to row her from island to island to graze on small patches of grass. These were the counterpoint to tragic shipwrecks, such as the *Algoma* and *Monarch,* that crashed into Isle Royale during raging blizzards.

How can an author fail with a cast of characters composed of voyageurs, Indians, miners, loggers, fishermen and wilderness mailmen? The drama of their work, the terror of shipwrecks and the intrigue of smuggling are but a few of the fascinating stories displayed against the most beautiful background in the world.

This book is an attempt to tell a few of those stories in paintings and supporting text. It's just a taste, a hint, a small part of the drama played out in the Lake Superior area during pioneer times. For some reason, the romance of the North Country during this period of Lake Superior history didn't attract the popular artists and authors. Perhaps they were all in the warmer climates of the Southwest documenting and romanticizing cowboys, Indians and the Pony Express; or, perhaps they, too, were distracted by the California Gold Rush, Davy Crockett at the Alamo or the long knives against Cochise and Sitting Bull. Or, perhaps the Civil War and the Spanish-American War kept their interests in other directions.

Where is the Lake Superior counterpart to Southwest artists such as Karl Bodmer, Jacob Miller, George Catlin, Charles Russell and Frederick Remington? True, Francis Hopkins and Peter Rindlisbacher helped us to better understand the voyageur era of the North Country. And Paul Kane left us with a few impressions on his way to the Canadian west coast in the mid-1800s. But their efforts weren't enough to capture the imaginations of the popular culture in the way that the artists and writers of the South and West did.

Someday the storytellers of books and film will turn their eyes away from the popular myths and explore the reality of this colorful cast of characters composed of voyageurs, loggers, fishermen, miners and ship captains who interacted in the drama across the North Country stage.

– Howard Sivertson

Coureurs de Bois

According to historian William Warren, the country surrounding Lake Superior has been the home of Ojibway people since about 1500. Leaving what is now called Sault Ste. Marie, they traveled west, some going north while others went south around the shore of the lake. The first record of white Europeans venturing into the area is of Catholic priests, explorers and the French *coureurs de bois* fur traders.

The first *coureurs de bois* who came to Lake Superior in the 1600s to trade with the Indians were independent fur traders traveling in bark canoes loaded with trade goods from Montreal and Michilimackinac. After a few years of trading, they paddled back home with their canoes loaded with valuable furs which they sold for high profits. In the late 1600s, the government of New France insisted on licensing the trade, imposing rules and regulations that reduced incentives for the *coureurs de bois.* Some traders decided to continue their trade illegally, without the expensive licensing, taxation and inhibiting controls. *Coureurs de bois,* or woods runner, became a derogatory term used to define the illegal trader, at least to government officials, while the term *voyageur* was used to describe the licensed trader.

Many of the voyageurs, financed and outfitted by traders in Michilimackinac, ventured north around Lake Superior to the Kaministiquia and Pigeon rivers which connected the vast beaver country of the Northwest to Lake Superior. By 1732, La Vérendrye's party, on its way to establish a trading post at Rainy Lake and Lake of the Woods, crossed over the Grand Portage that connected Lake Superior with the upper reaches of the Pigeon River.

There were Ojibway settlements along the Boundary Waters in the late 1730s, and it wouldn't be stretching anyone's imagination to believe that Indians from Saganaga Lake might travel south in August to harvest blueberries and to fish along the Magnetic River between Gunflint Lake and Saganaga Lake. It's quite likely that the voyageurs and *coureurs de bois* traded with the Indians along the way.

The French voyageur and Ojibway got along well, and marriages between the two cultures were common. Descendants of these families were among the first settlers of the early Lake Superior communities who helped shape the character of those to follow.

Campsite at Day's End

The era of the *coureurs de bois* came to an end when the English took Canada away from the French in 1763. The American Revolution followed soon after, forcing loyal English and Scottish subjects to leave the American colonies and cross the St. Lawrence River into Canada. Men like Alexander Henry and the Frobishers were quick to revive the fur trade that had lain dormant during the French and Indian War, adopting the French trading methods and the French Canadian voyageur canoemen. After a few years of intense competition and dwindling profits, a group of Scottish traders joined forces and created the famous North West Company.

The North West Company established a trading post in the geographic center of their trade route, between their warehouses in Montreal and the vast beaver country of northwest Canada. Grand Portage was the hub of the company trade from 1783 until 1803, when it was moved to the mouth of the Kaministiquia River across the border in Canada.

Smaller company trading posts throughout Canada gathered furs from the natives during the fall and winter seasons. When the waterways were free of ice in the spring, the northern voyageurs, called "Northmen," loaded their 26-foot bark canoes with furs and started their long journey to Grand Portage, rendezvousing with the canoe brigades from Montreal.

The work was hard and grueling – paddling and carrying tons of furs across lakes and over portages for 18 hours a day with little time for rest. Some canoes came from as far away as the Rocky Mountains and Lake Athabaska, traveling for six weeks to Rendezvous.

Around sunset each night, the hardy voyageurs would stop at a campsite, similar to the Saganaga Lake campsite pictured, to eat their supper and rest for the evening. The canoes were unloaded, carried ashore and tipped on edge to create shelter under which paddlers slept.

Although the Scotsmen were not as likely to intermarry with the Indian women as the French canoemen, some did take native wives and raised families. Their descendants were also part of the cultural history of the Lake Superior settlements whose roots stemmed from the fur trade.

Portaging Around Saganaga Falls – 1795

The annual summer Rendezvous in July was highly anticipated by voyageurs, Indians, the North West Company partners and clerks alike. Although Rendezvous was a time for hard work, it was also a time of great celebration. The fun began after the company partners conducted their annual meeting and the tons of trade goods and furs had been re-sorted and packed. It was the best of times for voyageurs.

After spending a bleak, cold winter at their North Country posts with the twin threats of starvation and freezing, the Northmen looked forward to the regale at Rendezvous.

The voyageurs from Montreal were generally younger and less experienced than the more seasoned and professional Northmen. The young men from Montreal were eager for a summer's adventure away from pious parents and clergy. After unloading trade goods and supplies at Grand Portage and carrying their cargo over the 8½-mile portage to Fort Charlotte, the voyageurs from Montreal joined the fun and games of Rendezvous.

As many as 1,000 men celebrated with food, wine, women and song on any given day during the summer Rendezvous at Grand Portage. But too soon it was over. The Montreal canoes were loaded with furs. The voyageurs were anxious to return to Montreal before the St. Lawrence River froze, which would delay the shipment of furs to Europe. Northbound canoes, loaded with trade goods and supplies, headed north, scheduled to arrive at wintering posts before the waterways froze.

More than a thousand miles of rivers, lakes and portages had to be crossed by many of the canoe brigades heading north. Short portages, much like the Saganaga Falls portage pictured, were relatively easy, compared to many longer carries along the way. Canoes were unloaded onto shore, carried around the falls, set in the water and reloaded again. The company partners, trading post managers and clerks traveled in relative comfort, while the voyageur canoemen did all the work.

In 1821, the Hudson's Bay Company absorbed the North West Company. With more efficient trade routes through Hudson Bay, furs and trade goods no longer had to be shipped through the Boundary Waters and across Lake Superior. However, 36-foot express canoes, carrying company officials between Fort William and Sault Ste. Marie, continued to be a part of the Lake Superior scene until 1882.

Boat Day at Ransom Mine – 1847

Although the voyageur express canoes of the Hudson's Bay Company continued to traverse Lake Superior in the 1830s, the once powerful fur trade was in decline. The American Fur Company that took over the fur trade on the American side of the border after the War of 1812 also suffered from the lack of demand and the growing scarcity of furs.

Ramsey Crooks, new owner of the American Fur Company, tried commercial fishing from various stations around the lake and at Isle Royale from 1835 to 1842. His small fleet of sailing ships, which included the *John Jacob Astor, William Brewster, Siskawit* and *Madeline,* were about the only ships of any size on Lake Superior at that time. After the company's failure in 1842, the ships had either sunk or were sent to the lower lakes, leaving Lake Superior nearly devoid of large ships, except for the 54-foot schooner *Algonquin.* She was the first ship to be dragged by horses across the Sault Ste. Marie portage in 1839 and launched in Lake Superior to carry passengers, mail and freight between the settlements along the shores. She also served the new copper mining communities of Isle Royale from 1843 to 1855, bringing in supplies and hauling out copper.

In the painting "Boat Day at Ransom Mine," I tried to capture some of the excitement of the infrequent visits of the *Algonquin* to Isle Royale. Irish, Scandinavian and Cornish miners hiked miles of trails from other mining locations around the island to meet the boat. Voyageur and Indian commercial fishermen sailed Mackinaw schooners from distant fisheries to rendezvous with the *Algonquin,* depending on her to ship fish and deliver supplies.

Miners' wives and families at the Ransom Mine dressed up for the celebration of meeting the boat. I'm sure boat day was a holiday for all the residents of Isle Royale, as they congregated on the dock at Ransom townsite to get long-awaited letters and parcels from friends and relatives on the mainland. They also picked up groceries and other supplies to tide them over for several months until the next trip.

After the opening of the Sault Locks in 1855, larger ships, side-wheelers and the new propeller-driven steamships arrived on Lake Superior, beginning a new era of regularly scheduled water transportation to supply the needs of the growing communities around the lake.

Copper mining on Isle Royale failed in 1855. New attempts to mine copper also failed in the 1870s and 1890s, putting an end to the dream of mineral riches on Isle Royale.

An Angel Descends on Isle Royale

The Panic of 1837-1841 put an end to the fishing operations of the American Fur Company on Isle Royale. A few Indians and ex-voyageurs continued to fish from the abandoned AFC fisheries. In 1843, mining exploration began on the island for the copper deposits presumed to exist by historical fact and legend. The main rush began in 1846, when miners became established in the Rock Harbor and Todd Harbor areas.

Many of the miners were Irish Catholics whose spiritual needs were the responsibility of the Catholic priest who served the wilderness area of Lake Superior's North Shore from Grand Portage to Prince's Bay (Thunder Bay) and Isle Royale. Transportation among his widely dispersed flock was by whatever kind of boat or canoe the good Father could borrow from his parishioners, most of whom were natives living on the North Shore. One of the little known but adventurous Jesuit priests was Father Nicholas Fremoit, who, from 1848 to 1852, taught religion and administered the sacraments to the Indians and the Irish miners at Silver Islet and Isle Royale.

In his "Lettres des Nouvelle Mission du Canada," Father Fremoit recorded several dangerous crossings to Isle Royale in a birch-bark canoe with Indian paddlers. His travels across the open lake to Isle Royale were fraught with danger – often requiring heroic effort from his "Savages," who paddled him and the frail bark canoe through violent winds and enormous waves, sometimes in the black of night, with little to guide them but his constant prayers. He expressed his thankfulness upon reaching the island's shores, safe and sound after nearly swamping and foundering in the tremendous waves.

Father Fremoit traveled from mine locations at Todd Harbor to Snug Harbor, Siskiwit and Ransom Mine where he improvised an altar, said Mass, heard confessions and baptized the infants. On one occasion his native guide became the godfather *and* the godmother to an isolated Irish couple's baby.

Father Fremoit slept under his canoe on the hard ground in all kinds of weather, wrapped in a buffalo robe and blankets. Occasionally he would be marooned and his food supply would run out. He would have suffered severely if his parishioners hadn't come to the rescue with food and lodging.

Father Fremoit claims to have been as welcome as "an angel from Heaven" on those infrequent trips to his island flock. Among the gifts received by the Father were a beautiful live rooster and hen to populate his hen house on the mainland.

I tried to capture the spirit of joy and thanksgiving of Father Fremoit, after crossing 20 miles of cold, storm-tossed Lake Superior to the warmth and shelter of Todd Harbor on Isle Royale. I'm sure he thanked God for answering his prayers and for the miracle of a safe crossing. The Indians who paddled and managed the fragile craft the entire way may have felt they deserved some praise, too, but it isn't evident that they received it from the good Father.

Daring Rescue During the Famine of 1856

Superior City was in its infancy in 1855, and her twin port Duluth had not yet been named. The Merritt, Ely and Wheeler families were among the early pioneers who settled at the head of the lakes just prior to the Indian Treaty at La Pointe in 1854, which opened property along Lake Superior's North Shore for settlement by the whites. Surveyors and prospectors were among the first to inhabit the area, anxious to stake their claims on the rich gold, silver, copper and iron ore deposits that they believed existed.

Superior City was isolated in those days, with only a footpath to St. Paul. Almost all supplies and people came from Sault Ste. Marie by infrequent and unscheduled ships, which left the settlement totally isolated during the winter. Late fall storms that prevented the last shipment of winter supplies to the community were disastrous, threatening the settlement with starvation.

In December 1855, surveyor Robert McLean and friend W.W. Kingsbury learned of a flour shortage in Superior City. This was an indicator of a general food shortage, which could result in a famine before spring. The first shipload of supplies would not be delivered via the lake until May, which would be too late.

McLean and Kingsbury heard a rumor that the trading post at Grand Portage had flour to spare. Deciding to risk the perils of freezing to death or drowning, they rowed their 18-foot boat 300 miles, round-trip, to bring back as much flour as the boat could carry.

They set off in January 1856, the coldest month of the year. Below-zero temperatures created a phenomenon called frost smoke over the waters of the still-open lake. Ice crystals, caused by extremely cold air meeting the relatively warm water, rose in wispy columns hundreds of feet into the air, restricting visibility to almost zero. Splashing water from the wind-tossed waves coated the boat with ice, inside and out. To keep warm and to stay alive, they rowed constantly along the lonely, isolated North Shore until they reached Grand Portage.

Four barrels of flour were purchased from Mr. Elliott, a clerk at Mr. McCullough's trading post, and once again the pair set out to row the heavy load home. They dropped one barrel off at the small settlement of Beaver Bay, whose inhabitants were in the same predicament. The other three barrels were distributed to their neighbors at Superior City.

Some say the rescue was profit-motivated. Having purchased the flour at $16 per barrel and selling it for $60 per barrel, McLean and Kingsbury earned a net profit of $192 for their trouble. We can only decide that for ourselves. I suggest that each of us make a similar trip some January to gain a better perspective before deciding.

H. Sivertson
© 1992

The Schooner *Charley* En Route to Prince Arthur's Landing

Taking advantage of a fresh southwest breeze, the schooner *Charley* scoots wing 'n wing through the Susie Islands on her way from Beaver Bay to Prince Arthur's Landing. She's carrying mail, supplies and a load of lumber from the Wieland Brothers Sawmill at Beaver Bay. Some of her cargo is lumber for building the new mining town of Silver Islet on the Sibley Peninsula and timbers for the mine. It's possible she is also carrying supplies for the Dawson Road being constructed from Prince Arthur's Landing to Winnipeg to carry Colonel Wolsely's 60th Rifles on their way to quell the Riel Rebellion at Fort Gary.

Captain Albert Wieland, a recent German immigrant, is shouting orders to his crew aboard the *Charley* in three different languages: German, English and Ojibway. Albert and his four brothers immigrated from Germany after the European Revolution in 1848. Some of the Wieland family arrived in 1856 at Beaver Bay aboard the side-wheeler steamer *Illinois*. They came looking for minerals and settled in the New Frontier.

Within six weeks after their arrival, the Wieland families, with several other German and Swiss families, had built seven houses and two shanties, cleared 12 acres of land and planted four, built seven miles of road and cut 12 tons of hay. They'd come to stay.

The Wieland brothers built a sawmill to provide lumber for building the town. They continued logging and sawing and shipped the surplus lumber to Ontonagon, Marquette and other Michigan towns. The growing town of Port Arthur required enough lumber to support a Wieland office and lumber yard in the new city, as did the new town of Duluth.

The 63-foot schooner *Charley* was purchased by the Wielands to deliver lumber to customers around the lake. Her crew consisted of German and English settlers and the Ojibway who lived at Beaver Bay. Names of succeeding captains and crew members are a who's who of early North Shore dignitaries: Captain Holmgren, Chief John Beargrease, John Morrison, Antoine Mashowah, Jack Scott and Captain Peterson.

The schooner *Charley* was an integral part of the development of the new and growing settlement along the shores of Lake Superior, until she was destroyed by a storm that smashed her on the rocks at Beaver Bay.

The only visual documentation I could find of the *Charley* was a tiny suggestion of the schooner anchored in the harbor in an early painting by school teacher J.J. Lowry. There is conflicting information regarding actual dimensions, but it is generally agreed that she was about 63 feet long and 50 gross tons. The *Charley* in the painting is my interpretation.

Columbia, the First Ore Boat

What a majestic sight the brigantine *Columbia* must have been sailing along the shore of Lake Superior in 1855. To my knowledge, she was the only brigantine to have sailed the lake's waters until 1855. Her foremast sported square sails, giving her an unusual appearance to the few humans used to seeing only schooners and sloops sailing the wilderness waters.

Lake Superior was a relatively desolate lake before the locks at Sault Ste. Marie opened in 1855, with very few ships of any size being seen.

After the War of 1812 and the decline of the fur trade, shipping traffic decreased. The American Fur Company's small fleet of sloops and schooners left Lake Superior by 1842 when the company fishing venture failed.

Seven schooners and two steamers, hauled by horses across the portage at Sault Ste. Marie between 1839 and 1845, were the only vessels on the lake to service copper mining ventures.

The schooner *Algonquin* came across in 1839. In 1845, the schooners *Ocean, Fur Trader, Chippewa, Florence, Swallow* and *Merchant* followed along with two steamer propellers, the *Independence* and the *Julia Palmer*. But these were not enough to serve the promising mining industry, destined to bring hordes of workers and settlers to occupy the roadless wilderness around the lake.

Although not the first ship through the newly opened Soo Locks, the 91-foot brigantine *Columbia* was the first ship to carry iron ore from the new mines at Marquette, Michigan, to steel mills on the lower lakes. The 132 tons of red ore, loaded on her deck by shovel and wheelbarrow, was the first bulk shipment of ore through the canal on August 17, 1855 – just two months after the lock opened.

The opening of the locks at the Soo changed the Lake Superior country forever, loosing the great passenger ships from the lower lakes to carry immigrants and freight to Lake Superior's burgeoning settlements. Steamships carrying iron ore, coal and wheat soon followed, making Lake Superior ports the largest in tonnage in the United States. Cruise ships of the tourist trade carried vacationers on adventure tours, swelling the ship traffic on Lake Superior.

But I imagine the most thrilling sight of all was the appearance of the little brigantine *Columbia*, with all her sails unfurled before the wind, coming over the empty horizon of Lake Superior in 1855.

A Letter from Norway

From 1856 until 1900, "Rowboat Express" along the North Shore made the "Pony Express" of the Southwest look like child's play. Heroic mailmen rowed small boats loaded with mail along the most dangerous 400-mile route in the world for almost 50 years. The Pony Express lasted only 18 months. Although the Rowboat mailmen didn't face hostile Indians along the way, they faced Lake Superior storms capable of sinking 1,000-foot ships. Frost smoke, fog and weather that was cold enough to ice down boats were other common hazards. The mail route was from Superior, along the North Shore to Pigeon Bay and across the lake to Isle Royale and back.

The mail was delivered sporadically until the 1870s, when an increase in settlers demanded regularly scheduled service with deliveries twice a month. Fishermen, farmers, trappers, miners and loggers were among the first pioneers to settle along the North Shore. Scandinavian immigrants came to fish and built their fish houses and homes at any nook or cranny along the shoreline that offered protection from lake storms. John Beargrease, Sam Howenstine, Jack Scott, Louis Plante and Joseph Montferrand were among the mailmen who connected the settlers' lives to the outside world – and especially to the "old country."

The painting "A Letter from Norway" shows the mail being delivered in January to one of the fishing families along the 400-mile (round-trip) route. The below-zero temperature causes frost smoke to rise, limiting visibility. Ice has to be chopped off the boat regularly to keep it from sinking. Spray from waves collects in the rowboat, sometimes freezing the mailman's boots to the bottom.

He has a letter from a relative back home for the Norwegian couple waiting at the fish house. The letter is full of gossip and news about friends and relatives. News of church doings and political goings-on plus family plans and gardening results swell the envelope that came by clipper ship to New York, then by train to St. Paul, then by stagecoach to Duluth and Superior. The heroic mailman risks his life against the most dangerous lake in the world to row that letter to the anxiously waiting couple. The mailman continues on his journey to Isle Royale, picking up an answer to the letter from Norway on his return trip.

What was so important in that letter to risk a man's life to deliver it? You probably know the answer better than I.

Waiting Out a Northeaster

I'm sure there were nice days during mid-summer when a light breeze pushed the 16- to 18-foot rowboats under sail along the mail route to the North Shore and Isle Royale. Little effort was required of the mailman on those few balmy days of summer, with the boat scooting along before a fair breeze. Those moments might have been enjoyable, if it weren't for the anxiety of knowing that the weather might turn bad at any time. Even the foggy days of early summer were not too distressing since the mailman rowed or sailed his boat close to shore, always following the dim shoreline to the next fish house or settlement.

But the cold, miserable northeasters or southwesters mixed with rain or snow were another story. The sudden storms that roared down from the hills to the northwest were feared most of all. Those were the storms that came instantly, catching commercial fishermen off guard and blowing their small skiffs miles out into the lake, swamping their boats and claiming their lives. It was always a good idea to stay close to shore under the protection of the hills where the wind couldn't reach.

The late fall and winter blizzards in subzero weather were also life-threatening. Even if the cold weather didn't bring snow, the frost smoke obliterated all reference points along the shore, leaving the mailman feeling suspended in a swirling mass of ice crystals.

Most of the time, the mailman had a few minutes to seek shelter from any storms that built gradually. He could pull his rowboat out of the water onto a sand or gravel beach that was protected from the wind and seas. He turned the boat on its side to offer more shelter from wind, rain or snow. Firewood was gathered and kept dry under the boat, and a small fire was kept burning nearby. He might spend two or three days waiting for a storm to pass over.

I imagine a lot of his time was spent pacing the beach, watching the weather, gathering wood, smoking a pipe and thinking. It's quite possible that some of his thoughts were of less dangerous occupations in warmer climates. Maybe he considered going to work for the Pony Express where working conditions were more conducive to staying alive.

H. SIVERTSON
©1989

The Schooner *Pierpont* at Wright Island – 1866

By 1842, the American Fur Company closed its commercial fishing stations on Isle Royale. Some of the Indian and French Canadian voyageurs previously employed by the company continued to fish for themselves, selling some of their catch to the copper mining companies that were getting established on the island. The Smithwick Mine, Ohio and Isle Royale Company, Pittsburgh and Isle Royale and the Siskowit Mining Company employed several hundred fish-eaters in their operations from 1843 until 1855.

Some natives from the Pigeon River region fished at Grace Point, while other Indians and voyageurs moved into the abandoned fisheries of the American Fur Company at Siskiwit Bay, Fish Island, Rock Harbor and Todd Harbor. By 1866, a fishery was established on Wright Island for commercial production of fish oil, as well as for salting down trout, whitefish and siskowits for shipment to mainland markets. Siskowits, a very fatty trout species, were caught, boiled down in iron vats and their oil extracted. The barrels of oil were shipped to Marquette, Michigan, for use in pharmaceuticals and as a base for house paint.

Once or twice during the season, a schooner like the *Pierpont* would stop in to pick up the fish oil and salt-fish from around the island. *Pierpont* was one of the schooners that occasionally brought supplies of food, mail, salt and barrels to the island fishermen, then returned with barrels of fish oil and salt-fish for mainland markets.

The 90-ton *Pierpont* was a 98-foot schooner owned in 1866 by Richard Coburn and H.N. Wheeler of Superior City, Wisconsin. She carried freight, lumber, iron ore and fish from Lake Superior to ports on the lower lakes. Alfred Merritt, who later became famous as one of the Seven Iron Men of Minnesota, was a deck hand on the *Pierpont* in 1866. At this time, he was employed by H.N. Wheeler, who owned the Wheeler Saw Mill in Duluth. R.G. Coburn was the ship's master on this trip.

The painting shows *Pierpont* being loaded with salt-fish kegs and fish oil at Wright Island on Isle Royale. The pots for rendering the fish oil can be seen on the Point, just to the right of the ship.

Scandinavian immigrants began settling on Isle Royale in the 1880s and continued fishing during its heydays from the early to mid-1900s.

Isle Royale Light on Menagerie Island

Lighthouse keeper William Stephans hastily scribbled in his log on October 26, 1875 (just 36 days after the light was turned on for the first time): "Damp and cloudy....The ENE gale increased almost to hurricane (unintelligible) at its acme....At 7 a.m., the sea went clean over the tower (61-feet high). Rocks was throwed in and brock the window sashes on the south side of the house and washed lumber, wood and everything loose of the island...."

That wasn't the first or last documentation of a lake that created unimaginably huge seas to batter Lake Superior's shores, of course. The second keeper at Menagerie Island, John H. Malone, who kept the beacon lit from 1878 to 1893, recorded another raging storm to hit the island in 1880.

"Oct. 16, 1880 – Hail, snow and rain...a tempest NE....Lost boat....Boathouse, ways and dock. It was impossible to save anything. I don't believe a cat could go from the dwelling to the boat house....It hailed awful."

And, 10 years later, another Malone entry: "October 13, 1890 – The sea today washed clean over the island – the whole length of the island."

Besides surviving lake storms, keeping the light lit and other operational and maintenance duties, John Malone and wife, Julia, raised 12 children, a vegetable garden, cows and chickens on that almost barren rock island guarding the entrance to Siskowit Bay. For 32 years, the Malone family hunted rabbits, ducks and geese, angled for lake and speckled trout and stole sea gull eggs from nearby islands to supplement their food supply. They ate hundreds of gull eggs each season.

"May 17, 1886 – We got 357 gull eggs off the rocks at Siscowette Point – 7 miles from the Lighthouse (today)." They had collected 1,478 eggs by June 1 that year.

Other entries documented their attempts at "rock farming," including: "June 3, 1886 – This is the first summer that we undertook to raise vegetables on the island – Our lettuce and radish are looking fine."

And: "August 5, 1887 – Some animal carried off 15 little chickens and killed two hens."

There were several shipwrecks that occurred within a stone's throw of the lighthouse, which kept the Malones from the boredom you might expect in the isolated environment of Menagerie Island.

The wreckage of the Canadian steamer *Algoma* floated by the lighthouse on November 9, 1885, after that ship crashed into Isle Royale in a violent snowstorm. The tug *George Hand* was wrecked on Schooner Island Reef in 1886. The *A.B. Taylor* provided entertainment for several days in 1890 as the Malones watched attempts to drag her off another reef near the light.

The shipwrecked freighter *Centurion* in 1895, the *Harlem* in 1898 and the bulk carrier *Bransford* in 1909 all had reefs named after them adjacent to the lighthouse established for their protection.

Lighthouses played a dramatic role as navigational aids on Lake Superior, but it does seem strange that so many shipwrecks occurred around the base of these lights after they were built. Maybe, like moths, ships are attracted to lights.

Musher Mail

Just a handful of settlers and a few prospectors inhabited the North Shore from Superior City to the Pigeon River between 1854 and 1870. Even so, the government authorized a post office at Beaver Bay in 1856 with Thomas Clark as postmaster. From Superior City to trading posts at Grand Portage and Pigeon River and mining camps at Isle Royale, mail was delivered using rowboats and sailboats from ice-out in April until freeze-up in February. Toboggans pulled by dog teams ran the unscheduled trips along the frozen lake during February and March.

Settlers began arriving in greater numbers and, by 1873, a post office was established in Grand Marais to help serve the growing communities along the North Shore. Men like Robert McLean, Albert and Henry Wieland, John Beargrease (both senior and junior), George Ward, Samuel Montferrand and Louis Plante were among the heroic mailmen who delivered the mail for more than 50 years.

Some notes from Dr. Willis Raff's book *Pioneers in the Wilderness* tell the story: "Day and night, good weather or bad made no difference to John (Beargrease). He was sure to arrive sometime with the mail intact. He was known to travel day and night without food and when he reached his journey's end with his faithful dog team, they would all rest up for a short while and start on the return trip regardless of weather conditions. He and his dogs were known to be snowbound for days at a time, but they would finally come through tired, hungry and frost-bitten. But nature's wild winter blasts had no terror for faithful John."

The bells commonly hung on the dogs' collars were primarily used to frighten off wolves, but also announced the approach of the long-awaited mail. "On cold winter evenings, the dog sled bells could be heard for miles before they arrived.

"Louis Plante arrived from Grand Portage on Monday with the first dog train of the season and with his trained tandem dogs, jingling sleigh bells…resembled old Santa Claus coming to town…."

There were lots of horror stories about nearly freezing to death; about breaking through thin ice on frozen bays and almost losing dogs, mail and mailman; and about encounters with blizzards and shifting ice packs. But the mail usually went through.

By 1900 the wagon road was completed from Duluth to Grand Marais, and then to Pigeon River several years later. Winter mail was then hauled by horses and sleighs, except for the one season that John Beargrease used his steel toboggan.

The Herring Choker

The Scandinavian herring fishermen who immigrated to the North Shore in the late 1800s were called "herring chokers" because of the way they squeezed herring from their gill nets. By simultaneously squeezing the herring with one hand while twisting and pushing with the other, the small, silver fish were "picked" from the entangling meshes at the rate of one fish every few seconds.

Each morning, weather permitting, the North Shore fisherman pushed his wooden skiff into the water from the slide next to his fish house and rowed to his gill nets set offshore within a mile or two from his landing. A gill net resembles a tennis net, suspended a few fathoms under the water's surface running perpendicular to the shoreline. One gill net is about 300 feet long and about seven feet deep with meshes about two inches square. Several 300-foot nets tied together, end to end, make a "gang." Each gang was suspended by a series of floats to varying depths, depending on how deep the fishermen anticipated the fish would be swimming. Each end of the "gang" was anchored to the bottom of the lake with several burlap coffee sacks filled with gravel and marked by a floating buoy.

The herring choker pulled the net in on one side of the boat and reset it on the other side, picking out the herring as he went. He might get five pounds or five tons, depending on the season and the movement of fish. Most of the herring in the early days would be salted down in 100-pound kegs or frozen. In later years they were sold "fresh" to local markets. The herring, or blue fin, is a tasty fish, usually between 12 and 14 inches long, and commonly eaten fried, boiled, salted, pickled or smoked.

Herring fishermen were on the lake every day, as long as it was free of ice and the weather was not stormy. Although summer was a pleasant time to fish on the lake, the fishing was relatively unproductive. Fall was the best fishing, but the winds usually made it risky. Winter and subzero temperatures caused the greatest hardship on the fisherman, as his hands, swollen and numb from the cold water and freezing air, tried to untangle the fine meshes from the slippery fish. To keep his hands from freezing in the freezing temperatures, the fisherman often immersed them in the relatively warmer lake to thaw them out. He dressed most of the year in wool clothes and oil skins or rubber rain gear.

The storms of late fall and winter could be deadly, sweeping the fisherman to sea, swamping his small boat or leaving the unfortunate herring choker frozen to his oars.

Fisherman's Homestead

The sons and daughters of Norway, Sweden, Denmark and Finland came to fish in the late 1800s.

They established homes in every niche along the rugged shoreline that provided shelter for their fish houses and skiff slides. By 1920 there was a fisherman's "place" almost every half mile from Duluth to the Canadian border.

They fished for lake trout and whitefish, but primarily fished for herring. At first, log homes were built a short distance back from the shoreline, providing protection from the cold lake winds. Fish houses, where they processed the fish and stored their skiffs, were built at shore's edge next to their slides. Sometimes a net house was built nearby to store nets, salt, kegs, boxes and miscellaneous fishing gear. Several net reels were constructed for drying and repairing nets.

The best herring fishing was in the fall, the lake's stormiest season. Herring gill nets, set up to a mile offshore, provided up to 10,000 pounds of the 12- to 14-inch silvery fish each day during the peak of the "fall run." Strong winds and heavy seas made it difficult, at times impossible, to launch their 16- to 18-foot dory-like wooden skiffs into the lake. Landing the herring-laden skiffs back onto the skid or slide without broaching and swamping in heavy seas was oftentimes dangerous, if not impossible.

The fisherman in the painting is fortunate to have help on shore. His partner is waiting on the slide with a hook-on-a-cable running to a homemade capstan-like winch. The instant the skiff hits the slide, the partner will grab the skiff and jam the hook into its bow eyebolt, while the young lad at the capstan starts winching up the boat by pushing on the long lever. Waves start breaking over the stern of the skiff as both men run to the winch to haul the boat up the slide before she swamps and they lose all their herring. The whole family helps by back-splitting and salting down the tons of herring in 100-pound kegs. Schoolwork and housework suffer for a week or more as everyone gets involved in the herring run.

During the pre-road days, the herring kegs were loaded into skiffs and rowed out to meet the freight boats from Duluth – muscled aboard at sea. The herring were repacked by fish companies in Duluth and shipped to markets around the country, feeding people from North Dakota to New York. Providing food for America's tables was hard and dangerous work.

Henry Redmeyer Building the *Emilie*

The headline of the Duluth *Weekly Herald* on the 21st of November 1894 read "Suspected of Smuggling," which marked the beginning of the end for the beautiful 65-foot fishing schooner *Emilie*. The schooner was hand-built by Henry Redmeyer at Cross River, just four years prior to the false accusation.

Henry Redmeyer, with wife and son, Headly, settled at the mouth of the Cross River in 1880, building a home, commercial fishery and post office. He and his son built the *Emilie* from scratch, cutting white pine off his land and milling the lumber by hand. His only cost was $80 for nails for the 65-foot, 35-ton schooner. His dream ship would take him to fishing grounds around the lake for months at a time.

Many of the Scandinavian immigrant fishermen built their own herring skiffs, like the one shown directly in front of the fish house. A few were capable of building Mackinaw boats, like the one in the lower left. They were small schooners from 20 to 30 feet long used for commercial fishing throughout the Great Lakes.

The small rowboat with sails, to the right, may also have been constructed by a commercial fisherman. It's quite possible that the sail-rigged rowboat, being welcomed ashore by the Redmeyer family, may have carried Burt Fesler on his census-taking trip along the North Shore and Isle Royale in 1890.

Although opium was legal and widely used in patent medicines at the time, it was thought to be smuggled across the U.S./Canadian border to avoid the $12 per pound duty. U.S. Customs agents theorized that a French commercial fisherman from Canada hid packages of opium on Isle Royale, where they presumed Redmeyer and the *Emilie,* commercial fishing around Isle Royale at the time, picked up the packages for delivery to U.S. customers. The *Emilie* was under surveillance until the Customs agents were sure of catching Redmeyer red-handed. They boarded *Emilie* at Two Island, towed her to Duluth, tore her apart and came up empty-handed. The *Emilie* was clean, but her reputation was smeared. Redmeyer lost ownership of this wonderful ship, which was dismantled in Duluth, for unknown reasons, by her third owner, M. Gasson.

The building of the *Emilie* and other boats by commercial fishermen were examples of the self-reliant character of early pioneers around Lake Superior's shores. The boat building tradition continued in fishing families like the Hills, Crofts, Linds, Danielsons, Obergs and Ronnings until the mid-1900s.

The *Algoma* Tragedy – November 7, 1885

Try to imagine the terror on that black morning of November 7, 1885. The screams of men, women and children mixed with the roar of mountainous seas in a howling blizzard as the steamer *Algoma* struck a reef off Greenstone Island on Isle Royale. Imagine, if you can, an all-steel ship almost as long as a football field and as tall as a three-story building being tossed about helplessly by waves in the dark hours before dawn. Then, the sudden shudder of the hull as it was ripped open and giant seas broke the "unsinkable" ship in half. The blizzard raged on through the cold black of night, as relentless seas crashed over the ship, tearing off the cabins and superstructure on the top deck in just minutes.

Passengers and crewmen were swept into the water. Lifeboats were capsized while attempting to reach shore only 70 feet away, drowning some of the passengers within only a few feet of reaching safety. Those who reached shore alive watched through the night as the constant pounding of huge seas made rescue impossible for the few survivors huddled in the stern of the *Algoma*. The storm continued until the next night. When the seas finally subsided, commercial fishermen from the island rescued the survivors. Only 14 of the 61 passengers and crew survived, making it the worst shipwreck in Lake Superior's history at that time.

The 262-foot *Algoma* had been built just two years before in Scotland for the Canadian Pacific Railway. She was 1,773 gross tons, 38 feet in beam and 23 feet in depth, and was regarded as unsinkable because of her watertight compartments. Besides her freight capacity, she had accommodations for 130 passengers in first-class and 20 in steerage.

On her maiden voyage from Scotland, the *Algoma* sailed across the Atlantic from Scotland to Montreal. There she was cut in two and towed through the short St. Lawrence Canals, Lake Ontario and the Welland Canal to Buffalo, where she was reassembled for the journey to her new home port at Owen Sound. Her mission for the Canadian Pacific Railway was to carry supplies and immigrants from Owen Sound to Port Arthur, there to be shipped west by rail.

She left on her fateful trip from Owen Sound on November 5, 1885, passed through the locks the next day and continued into a ferocious gale the night of November 6. By the morning of the 7th, the gale had turned to a blizzard out of the northeast. Heavy seas and northeast winds drove the *Algoma* dangerously close to Isle Royale. With zero visibility, Captain Moore decided to turn back to where he thought was open lake, but the stern hit the reef off what is now called Mott Island, turning a horrible night into a worse night of horrors.

Gunflint City – 1893

Iron ore was discovered on the eastern edge of the Mesabi Range near Gunflint Lake 16 years earlier than on the famous west end of the Mesabi. Dreams of striking it rich north of Grand Marais included speculation about ore docks in Grand Marais harbor and railroads to Duluth.

In 1887, John Paulson started sinking ore shafts along the Kekekabic Trail just east of today's Gunflint Trail. The Port Arthur, Duluth and Western Railroad (Pee Dee) started laying track to the Paulson site in 1884 to carry the "unlimited" supply of rich ore to Port Arthur and the waiting ships at the newly constructed ore docks. Hundreds of men swarmed the woods trying to develop the Paulson mine in time to coincide with the railroad's arrival.

Gunflint City, built near the mine, consisted of a horse barn, dynamite house, ice house, tool house, shelter for steam engines, boilers and winches, mess hall with kitchen, and cabins and bunkhouses for the men. Last, but not least, a saloon and boarding (sporting) house for the "amusement and comfort of miners" was provided and operated by the famous Port Arthur madame, "Meg" Mathews.

Stockholders of the railroad and mining ventures were highly optimistic. Intelligent, rich, thoughtful men headed the operation. Surely they were thorough in researching and estimating the amount and quality of the ore available before putting their time, money and reputation on the line. Surely men like that wouldn't try to raise money by making exaggerated and outrageous claims in advertising, or would they?

In June 1893, the *Pee Dee* made its first trip to Gunflint City for its first and last load of ore. The painting shows Meg waving good-bye to the engineer of the *Pee Dee,* who salutes her with three toots on his whistle. He's towing one flat car with enough Paulson Mine ore to manufacture one pony-sized horseshoe. There was far more iron in the miners' tools than was brought up the shafts.

Three months later the mine was put up for sale, and some major investors went bankrupt. The railroad trestle across Gunflint Narrows burned in 1894, putting the American side of the railroad out of commission with no plans to rebuild. I'd guess that Meg moved on and did as well as could be expected.

I hiked through the woods with historian Bill Raff and found Gunflint City overgrown with trees and brush, with just a few mounds and indentations in the ground to indicate where the 19 structures once stood. I had to deduce the function of each structure. The painting is a result of those deductions.

John Beargrease and the Steel Toboggan – 1898

The number of pioneers along the North Shore increased from 1870 to 1900 as Scandinavian immigrants settled on the shore to take up commercial fishing and logging. Mining was still a glint in the eyes of an ever increasing number of mineral prospectors. As the communities grew, so did the demands for more mail, resulting in heavier loads on toboggans and rowboats.

The steamer *Hiram Dixon* started delivering the mail along the North Shore and to Isle Royale in 1890 and replaced the rowboat delivery, at least from April to December. Rowboats still carried the mail in the winter months of December until mid-February. Then the dog teams with toboggans took over until the steamships started again toward the end of April.

When loads got too heavy for the toboggans, John Beargrease designed his not-so-famous steel toboggan to carry more than a ton of mail and freight along the dog trail from Two Harbors to Grand Marais. The new contraption was eight feet long, three feet wide and one foot deep. The 360-pound steel toboggan was equipped with three steel runners to prevent slippage on the ice and snow. John's famous four-dog team was replaced by two horses named Red Charlie and White Charlie, who towed the steel toboggan from Two Harbors to Grand Marais until 1899, when the new wagon trail was finished. The new lakeshore wagon trail from Duluth to Grand Marais allowed winter and summer travel by horse-drawn stagecoach and sleigh, putting an end to the mailman career of John Beargrease.

John's father, Mokquabemmette (Beargrease), was the chief of a band of Indians who lived in Beaver Bay. He was one of the first mailmen on the North Shore, delivering with rowboats, dog sleds and the schooner *Charlie* from the 1850s until the 1870s. He was a tall, stately character who had many wives. He usually wore a blanket, was bare-chested and sometimes wore one of Mrs. Henry Wieland's outworn bonnets on his head. She gave the bonnets to Beargrease for his wives, but he insisted on wearing them.

John Beargrease Jr. ran the mail during the 1880s and 1890s. When the combination of lake steamer and stage road put him out of business, John returned to his previous business of fur trading with the Indians until his death in 1910. He is buried in his hometown of Beaver Bay.

Although the steel toboggan was used for only one year, it made a great impression on the pioneers who never forgot the sound of John's voice yelling orders to the horses long before they came into sight. Was it just a coincidence that the last name of his horses, White "Charley" and Red "Charley," was the same as the schooner *"Charley"* that his father captained in the 1870s?

The *Dixon* Unloading Lumberjacks at Chicago Bay

By 1883, the Booth Packing Company of Duluth started running the *T.H. Camp,* a tug that picked up fish and delivered supplies from Duluth to Canada and Isle Royale. She was replaced by the 149-foot freight and passenger steamer *Dixon* in 1888 which two years later was awarded the mail contract.

Captain "Fog King" Hector guided the ship, offering first-class passenger accommodations twice a week along the North Shore to Isle Royale and back, when the steamship *America* succeeded her in 1902.

The whistle announcing the arrival of the *Dixon* sent joy to the hearts of the isolated pioneers as they rushed to meet her and collect mail, packages, freight and passengers. Boat day was a cause for celebration in the larger communities on deep water harbors like Grand Marais, where happy citizens, dogs and even a moose would gather to meet the boat.

The *Dixon* also made hundreds of shorter stops along the route, rendezvousing with individual commercial fishermen, loading and unloading just offshore from the fishermen's homes. Cows, horses and pigs were unloaded by making the animals walk the plank, dumping them into the water and forcing them to swim ashore.

The painting shows the *Dixon* pausing outside the fishing community at Chicago Bay (Hovland) to unload the mail, supplies and lumberjacks for the Pigeon River Lumber Company. It was fisherman August Brunes' responsibility to row his skiff out to meet the *Dixon* in the middle of the night to pick up mail, supplies and passengers on the *Dixon*'s arrival from Duluth. If the *Dixon*'s whistle didn't wake August, Captain Hector would shine the ship's searchlight ashore into August's bedroom window, which usually did the trick. August Brunes had one rule when ferrying his lumberjack passengers: "If anyone was drunk or rowdy, August threw him into the lake to swim ashore."

After being replaced by the Booth Company's steamship *America,* the *Dixon* was totally destroyed by fire while in the harbor at Michipicoten Island on August 18, 1903. It was sad news for old friends along the North Shore and Isle Royale who recalled all the happy times of boat day with the steamer *Dixon.*

White Pine Logging Along the Pigeon River – 1900

'Timbberrrr" was the call in the woods, echoed from Maine to Michigan, Wisconsin and finally, by the mid- to late 1800s, the white pine forests of Minnesota. In Maine, the loggers were called "shanty boys." As they moved westward, they were called "choppers," then "timbermen," "timberjacks" and in Minnesota "lumberjacks." The early "jacks" were French Canadians, Scotch and Irish. By the time the white pine logging peaked in Minnesota, around 1900, Scandinavians and Finns were in the majority.

Most lumberjacks were honest, hardworking, rugged men who migrated each October to the logging camps from summer jobs in southern and central Minnesota. Many were farmers who brought their horses with them and worked as skidders and teamsters, hauling the logs out of the woods.

The "wild and woolly" colorful characters who have become synonymous with the legendary lumberjacks were in the minority. They were the drifters who worked long enough to make a stake, then headed for the nearest town to blow it on wine, women and song, returning to camp only after they were "busted" or "broke." Their colorful reputations overshadowed the hardworking dependable lumberjacks who were the backbone of the industry.

The Wieland brothers of Beaver Bay were among the first loggers along the North Shore of Lake Superior, cutting pine for their sawmill that supplied the wood for building many of the towns around the lake. From 1898 to 1905, the Alger Smith Company and the Pigeon River Lumber Company harvested the last stands of Minnesota white pine along the Pigeon River watershed in northeastern Minnesota and northwestern Ontario. Logging camps, where the men lived and cut timber from October through March, were built adjacent to the timberstands.

Timber cruisers marked the trees to be cut, sawyers felled the trees with axes and two-man crosscut saws, swampers limbed the trees and cleared the roads for skidders who dragged the 18-foot logs to the skidway using one or two horses and skidding tongs. The logs were then loaded on sleighs by crosshauling, using a team of horses, two cant hook men and a top loader. The sleigh was then towed by a two- or four-horse team on an ice road to the landing on the Pigeon River, where the logs were stored, then floated down river to Pigeon Bay in spring.

Huge corrals or "rafts" of floating logs were assembled at Pigeon Bay and towed by steam tugs to sawmills in Ashland or Duluth. They were sawed into lumber and shipped around the Midwest to build the cities of our growing nation.

Pigeon River Log Drive – Early 1900s

The spring log drives on the Pigeon River were the most colorful and exciting phase of the logging industry. The Pigeon River was the only way of transporting the white pine logs out of the roadless watershed along the Minnesota/Ontario border. Dams were built on the river to control water levels, and sluiceways were constructed to guide the logs around the largest falls. The logs were rolled into the river during high water at spring break-up and started their journey to market down one of the wildest rivers ever used for driving logs. Because of the beating they took as they tumbled through rapids and over falls, the logs had to be cut two feet longer than normal so their battered "broomstick" ends could be trimmed off to standard size at the mill.

After the white pine era, stands of spruce, balsam, fir, jack pine and aspen were harvested by loggers for the paper industry pulp mills. In the 1920s and 1930s, trees for the pulp industry were cut in eight-foot lengths and sent down the Pigeon River in the spring log drives.

The river drivers were a special breed of lumberjack, skilled in the dangerous but exciting work of guiding the pulp logs down river. Log jams in shallow water and river bends had to be cleared quickly before all the logs coming downstream piled up behind them, causing a major jam and tying up the drive. Working afoot or in large bateaux-like skiffs, "jacks" with pike poles, cant hook, peaveys and dynamite worked to free the "key log" in the jam, allowing the mass of logs to continue on its journey to Pigeon Bay. Balance, agility and strength were required of the river drivers, who ran and jumped from log to floating log, clearing one jam after the other. They wore caulked boots for traction on slippery logs and wool clothes to keep them warm even while wet.

After the main drive was over, "rearing" was necessary to collect all the logs still jammed in shallow water and along the river banks. Men worked along the banks and from bateaux to push the last logs back into the river on their journey to the river mouth and the waiting booms in Pigeon Bay.

At the river mouth the pulpwood sticks drifted into a large, floating corral-like pen of huge boom logs chained together. More than 50 acres of pulpwood were confined in the raft and towed across the lake to Ashland, Wisconsin.

Our country's ever-increasing demand for paper products is still being met by modern lumberjacks using mechanized methods. The old, colorful lumber camps with the wild and woolly jacks are gone, but the risky work of supplying our country's increasing demand for wood and paper products continues.

Rafting Tug

If a log could talk, the trauma and drama of its journey from forest to market would keep even the most blasé audience spellbound. The story would start as the log is felled in mid-winter by axe and saw, then dragged through the snow to a landing, loaded on a sleigh, wrapped in chains and hauled to the river, where it is stacked on the ice or bank to wait out the cold winter until break-up in the spring. Then the log is poked and prodded with pike poles and peaveys until it rides bumping and banging over rapids and falls with thousands of other logs just like it, finally floating out into Pigeon Bay. The log's sigh of relief is shortlived as it finds itself corralled in an area the size of four football fields with four to seven thousand cords of fellow travelers.

Trapped in an enclosure formed by more than 450 sitka spruce logs, three feet thick by 22 feet long, chained end-to-end in a giant circle, the log is now part of a raft that will be towed at 1 mile per hour by a 140-foot steam tug to Ashland, Wisconsin, more than 100 miles and 100 hours away. If the weather is calm, the best experience will be boredom. A storm can change the mood drastically, but not for the better. Once in Ashland, the log is loaded on a railroad car and, if it is white pine, taken to a sawmill or, if it is a pulp stick, to a paper plant.

Sometimes, at great financial loss to the company, sudden storms with huge seas broke up the rafts, scattering the thousands of cords of logs across Lake Superior to either waterlog and sink or wash up on beaches where residents cut them for firewood or used them for building purposes. Many times strong winds would blow the slow-moving tug backwards. Even in good weather, at normal traveling speed, it seemed like days before a rafting tug would travel out of the sight and sound of someone living on shore.

The typical rafting tug would be owned by large lumber and paper companies like the John Schroeder Lumber Company or Consolidated Paper Company. They were generally 120 to 150 feet long, about 30 feet wide with steam or diesel engines. The large towing tug was usually accompanied by a smaller tug about 50 feet in length whose job was to ride herd on the raft under way, respond to emergencies or run to shore on errands. Although it was slow and ponderous, this was the most efficient way of getting logs to market.

A partial list of rafting tugs on Lake Superior from the late 1800s to mid-1900s includes the *Gladiator, Gettysburg, A.C. Van Raalte, G.E. Brockway, Ashland, Hilton, Crosby, Maxwell, Saugatuck, Brower, Ames, Traveler, Whalen, Puckasaw, Erna, Butterfield (Purves)* and *John Roen III.*

The colorful era of the rafting tug that used to blacken the skies with smoke and fill the air with the constant throb of its engines came to an end in 1972, when the *John Roen III* towed the last raft from Grand Marais, Minnesota, to Ashland, Wisconsin.

Snoose Moose

Tourism became a major industry on Lake Superior around the turn of the century. Hay fever sufferers sought relief in pollen-free fresh air. Well-to-do city folks sought adventure and recreation offered by a proliferation of cruise ships plying the Great Lakes. Even relatively small ships like the *Dixon,* whose primary mission was carrying mail, supplies and fish, had accommodations for a few passengers. Some of those passengers were locals traveling between the North Shore and Isle Royale settlements, while some were tourists on their way to resorts along the *Dixon*'s route.

There were no roads nor automobiles in those days, leaving ships as the only connection between wilderness settlers and the rest of the world. Telephones, radios, motion pictures, television, VCRs and Nintendoes were nonexistent. People entertained themselves and each other with music, dancing, visiting, church socials, hunting, fishing and so on. Children were good at entertaining themselves with skiing, sledding, fishing and playing many games handed down through the generations and those they made up themselves.

They also played with Charley Johnson's pet cow moose, who followed the children wherever they went, joining in the fun as best she could. Many of the children chewed snoose, a flavorful, sandy-textured tobacco that came in round cans about three inches in diameter and one inch deep. According to the ads, "Just put a pinch between cheek and gum for a heavenly treat." The kids shared their snoose with the moose, who loved it and got hooked on it. "She just couldn't get enough of that wonderful snuff (another name for snoose)." The moose followed the kids to the town dock on boat days to greet the mail boat *Hiram Dixon.* The passengers soon learned about the moose's tobacco habit and, anxious to see her perform, offered her a dip from their own Copenhagen cans.

The moose caught on fast. She soon learned to answer *Dixon*'s arrival whistle, proceeding to the dock every boat day, whether the children accompanied her or not. She begged passengers for snoose by nudging the round bulge of the snoose can in their pockets. She was almost always rewarded with a dip.

I'm not sure what happened to the moose. Whether snoose led her to other vices, I can't be certain. But I know it could never happen today with all the laws we have to regulate and protect ourselves and animals. She probably wouldn't have been sued in those days if she accidentally sneezed into the can and splattered the ladies' pretty dresses.

And thank goodness we have television and VCRs today to keep our children entertained, indoors and away from the evil influences of a snoose-chewing moose.

Farming with a Rifle

Why would anyone wish to immigrate to the hardships of wilderness living? And how did they survive? The professional mineral prospectors came to the North Shore in 1855, after a treaty with the Ojibway opened it to white settlements. They stumbled around the rugged environs for years with compass and pickax, looking for the mother lode of gold, silver, copper and iron ore without success. Others came north after the Civil War, looking for a peaceful life. Scandinavian immigrants came for logging, fishing and the promise of their own piece of land, a promise denied to them in the old country.

During the panic of 1893, folks came from the city with hopes of surviving better in the wilderness, where they could hunt, fish, trap, log and clear enough ground for a garden on land free for the taking. They also harbored the hope of discovering valuable minerals on their land which would eventually make them rich.

Scandinavians settling on the North Shore became commercial fishermen. Their cash crop was the herring, whitefish and trout harvested from Lake Superior with net, hookline and hard work. Some also logged the white pine and trapped fur-bearing animals during the winter. While summer gardens yielded fruits and vegetables, hunting caribou, moose and deer provided red meat for the table. The stately woodland caribou, the main source of meat for the early pioneers, were a common sight along Lake Superior's shores until the 1920s. The caribou moved north when moose and deer migrated into the area.

The pioneers who settled away from the lake found patches of dirt large enough to farm between the countless boulders. Hay was gathered from wild meadows to feed a horse or cow, if they could afford one. Oftentimes the women stayed on the "farm" with the children during the winter, while the men logged, hunted or trapped in the woods to raise cash for those things they couldn't provide with their hands. Surviving the harsh environment required living off the land, which might involve shooting caribou, moose or deer even when prohibited by game laws.

While trying to raise his large family, one Cook County farmer shot many deer to provide meat for the table. Everyone, including the law, knew he was doing it, but understood and looked the other way. Some "sportsman" from downstate reported the farmer shooting deer out of season, forcing the law to take action and arrest him. The judge, although sympathetic to the farmer's situation, confiscated his gun and reprimanded the farmer severely with a tongue-lashing, but then released him. The farmer pleaded for the return of his gun by asking the judge, "How do you expect me to farm in Cook County without my rifle?"

Trapping

One of the oldest professions in the New World is still practiced in the North Country today. Although on a steady decline since the heyday of the fur trade, trapping played an important role as a seasonal source of income for the early pioneers. Woodsmen like Sam Howenstein, Sam Zimmerman, Jack Scott, Benny Ambrose and a host of others had trap lines strung throughout the area north of Lake Superior to the Boundary Waters. This vast area of rivers and lakes provided habitat for beaver, lynx, marten, bobcat, otter, mink, fox, weasel, wolf, muskrat and bear. Their pelts brought a handsome price from fur buyers in Grand Marais, Duluth and Ashland.

The trap lines ran for miles through the wilderness. Trappers spaced their shacks about a day's journey apart to provide shelter at night. Canoes were used in early fall to run traps along lakes, rivers, and beaver dams, while snowshoes and dog sleds were the mode of travel between sets in the winter.

Charlie Johnson's Trading Post in Grand Marais purchased a lot of the furs from local trappers. But if the trappers became dissatisfied with the local price, they loaded the furs in their canoes and paddled a risky voyage across Lake Superior to Ashland, Wisconsin, as trapper Jack Scott was prone to do on occasion.

It was a lonely and, at times, dangerous life for the trapper, especially in winter when frozen hands and feet were common. Although attacks by wild animals were rare, Jack Scott had a run-in with a sow bear that nearly cost him his life. He literally stumbled over her while stepping over a windfall, surprising her as she was nursing her cub. The angry bear severely mauled Jack. Although he tried shooting her with his pistol pressed against her neck, the sow knocked the ineffective weapon into the snow. Just before falling unconscious from his wounds, Jack managed to pull his knife and slit her throat. Although his legs and chest were terribly torn by teeth and claws, he was somehow able to get back to his shack, where he recovered enough to crawl two miles through the woods to a road, where he was rescued. Friends went to where the scrap took place, finding the dead sow but no sign of the cub.

To add insult to injury, game wardens investigating the scene found that Jack was illegally trapping beaver. Jack was arrested, convicted and fined, which made him so angry that he never trapped again.

Tourism Begins on the North Shore

A little less than 50 years after the North Shore was opened to settlement by white miners, loggers, trappers and fishermen, tourism began. By the late 1890s, immigrant commercial fisherman C.A.A. Nelson was looking for a way to supplement his income from fishing and opened his Lutsen home to moose hunters and hay fever sufferers.

Thus, Lutsen Resort was the first resort on the shore. Charlie Nelson guided moose hunters and sport fishermen, while his wife, Anna, cooked, fed and pampered other guests seeking relief from hay fever or a healing environment for tuberculosis.

There were no roads accessing the area, so transportation was provided by the steamships *Dixon, America, Easton* and others plying the waters of Lake Superior. Hotels in Hovland, Grand Marais and Isle Royale sprang up to take advantage of the growing tourist trade coming from metropolitan centers around the Great Lakes. After the road was built along the shore, automobiles became the popular mode of transportation, eventually forcing the lake ships out of the tourist business.

Commercial fishermen along the shore built cabins to accommodate tourists now arriving by automobile. First came "rustic" cabins without plumbing, then the more serious operators modernized with indoor plumbing that transformed them into "modern" cabins.

One enterprising fisherman's wife talked her husband into converting the upstairs of his net house leaning over the water's edge into a "scenic tourist room." She moved the fishing paraphernalia to the ground floor, installed a bed, a nightstand with water pitcher and basin, hung curtains in the window and towels and wash clothes on a nail. Then, she put her sign on the road advertising "Waters Edge Tourist Room" and waited for that easy money to come rolling in.

She escorted her first guest up the ladderlike stairway to the cute, scenic room with the low ceiling above the net house. He stood stooped over, so as not to hit his head on the cobweb-festooned rafters, quickly surveying the situation.

"I see you don't have indoor plumbing," he said.

"Nope," she responded.

"How much?" he asked.

"Be $2.50 a night," she said.

"But," he protested, "I paid $2.50 for a modern room last night. For $2.50 I had a nice hot bath in luxurious surroundings."

She curtly countered in her Norwegian accent, "Vell, if you had a bath last night, you von't be needin' vun tonight."

Despite such modest origins, tourism is now the largest industry on the North Shore, Isle Royale and the Sawbill and Gunflint trails, as stressed-out city dwellers seek refuge in the relatively pristine, unspoiled environment of the north.

Boat Day

The steamer *America* was not the only ship hauling passengers, mail and freight along the North Shore and to Isle Royale in the early 1900s, but she was the favorite of the settlers along her route.

She was dependable and attentive to the needs of the folks who met her arrival every scheduled boat day. She was the first ship fast enough to make three scheduled round trips a week from Duluth to Port Arthur and Isle Royale.

From 1902 to 1928, she delivered passengers, mail and supplies and picked up mail, fish, raspberries and a few potatoes harvested along her route. Her palatial dining hall and gambling facilities entertained a mixed bag of passengers – from the hoity-toity to the rough and tumble.

Irregular boat service along the shore began with the small tug *T.H. Camp,* whose primary function was to service the commercial fishermen, dropping off supplies and picking up fish for market in Duluth. The *Hiram Dixon* began regularly scheduled trips in 1888 and serviced western Lake Superior communities until 1902.

Settlers along the shore in those early years would have been greeted with very different sights and sounds than those we experience today. Because the area was roadless until the early 1920s, schooners and steamships provided the most efficient and economical way to carry passengers and freight. A myriad of coal-burning steamships and tugs left a layer of black smoke suspended over the shipping lanes.

Sounds of horns, steam whistles and throbbing engines announcing their arrivals and departures were ever present in the hurly-burly of steamship traffic. The light-struck sails of three-masted schooners carrying lumber, iron ore and wheat broke the horizon as far as the eye could see.

Tourism encouraged more and more ships like the *America* into carrying passengers between resorts on Lake Superior and the lower lakes. Steamships like the *Easton, Bon Ami, Hunter, Argo, Isle Royale, Moore* and *Mabel Bradshaw* serviced communities around Lake Superior.

Huge luxury liners like the *North American, South American, Huronic* and *Noronic* carried tourists around the Great Lakes until the 1960s.

A navigation error at 2 a.m. on June 28, 1928, ended the *America's* career. Leaving Washington Harbor, she struck a submerged bank in the North Gap, between Thompson Island and the main island. Captain Smith tried to beach his sinking vessel in a small bay, but she foundered and sank in deeper water.

In 1965 a group purchased the sunken vessel and began efforts to refloat her. Long a favorite scuba diving site, hostile opposition quickly appeared. A mysterious explosion on the sunken vessel in April 1966 effectively ended that effort.

The long blasts of steam whistles announcing the arrival of grand ships are gone now, as is the joy of boat day along the North Shore. The giant lake is quiet. Lighthouses "peep" instead of "roar" at the fog. Giant ore boats swish silently through the water leaving no trail of soot in the sky. Even sports boats are relatively soundless, as they dart about entrances of harbors. But, to us old-timers, something is missing – like one color from the rainbow.

Abandoning the *Monarch* – 1906

There are conflicting reports on why the *Monarch* crashed against the palisades of Blake Point on Isle Royale and of the events that followed, but there are probably good reasons for the confusion. It could be that frozen navigational equipment during the raging blizzard in subzero weather in the black night had something to do with being off course. The terror, panic and confusion caused when your ship suddenly and unexpectedly slams into an unseen rock cliff, breaks in half and begins to sink could be the cause of conflicting viewpoints of the frantic events that followed.

On December 6, 1906, the 240-foot wooden passenger-freighter *Monarch* was on her last trip of the season, hauling grain, general cargo and 12 passengers from Port Arthur to Sarnia, Ontario. It was dark by the time they departed Thunder Cape, Ontario, and Captain Edward Robertson set his course for the channel between Passage Island and Blake Point on Isle Royale. The below-zero temperatures caused frost smoke to rise off the lake, and the light snow turned into a raging blizzard. Visibility was zero. High winds created heavy seas that crashed over the ship causing a build-up of ice on hull and deck.

About the time Captain Robertson predicted they'd be passing through the channel, the steamer slammed headlong into the shallow rocks just 25 feet from the palisades of Blake Point, about one mile off its intended course. The engineer kept the engine running and propeller turning to keep the ship from sliding off the reef into 100 feet of water. In just moments, the seas broke her in two and the stern section sank to the bottom.

A lifeboat was launched to carry a line to shore, but the seas were too large and the attempt failed. A long line was then tied to a wooden ladder and lowered over the bow with deck hand Jack McCallum standing on the ladder. He was swung like a pendulum until he could leap ashore with the line and scale the ice-covered rocks where he tied the line to a tree on the ledge. Thirty-one crewmen and 12 passengers crossed hand-over-hand on the hawser to safety ashore.

They built a fire and makeshift windbreak of branches. Canned salmon and flour from the wreck kept them from starving for the next two days. Rescue finally came after the third night, when the lighthouse keeper from Passage Island took a survivor aboard his rowboat and put him on a passing steamer for Port Arthur. Everyone, except one crewman who drowned, was rescued by the tug *James Whalen* on December 10, 1906.

The pride of the Canadian Northern Navigation Company was the victim of a frozen taffrail log, a malfunctioning compass and a bit of faulty judgment caused by almost impossible weather conditions.

The *Monarch* rests on the bottom of the lake next to Blake Point, where she can be visited by scuba divers.

The Mysterious Mosquito Fleet

Little is known about the boats of the Mosquito Fleet that swarmed over the lake in the early 1900s. They carried fish, gasoline and sometimes rutabagas along the roadless North and South shores of Lake Superior. Most of the Mosquito Fleet boats were in the 40- to 50-foot class, carrying about 20 tons of cargo each. Except for a few boats in the 110-foot class like the *Hazel* and *Swansea,* most looked much like the tug in the painting.

Their basic mission was to pick up salted, fresh and frozen herring from fishermen's homes along the lake, from Pigeon Point to Ashland, and deliver the herring to wholesale fish companies in Duluth. These boats were small enough to maneuver the small harbors and bays where the fishermen lived. The boats moved from fish house to fish house until they were fully loaded, then set sail for Duluth or Two Harbors. During the summer months, they carried fresh herring iced down in boxes or salted in kegs. Frozen herring was also shipped during the winter. Relatively large luxury passenger/freight ships like the *America, Argo* and *Hunter* preferred to carry only lake trout and whitefish, because herring took up more space than they were worth on those snobbish, palatial steamers. Occasionally, in addition to fish, the Mosquito Fleet carried rutabagas, potatoes and gasoline to fishermen along the route.

Most of the dozen or more tugs (no one knows how many for sure, but one old-timer estimated about 17) were privately owned by independent operators who worked on commission from the fish companies in Duluth. Some of the boats were built by the captains who operated them. The *Dagmar* was built by Chris Ronning, who had no previous boat-building experience. He merely laid the keel and made 'er up as he went along. The Axel Obergs, senior and junior, from Grand Portage owned and operated the *Red Wing, Elvina, Thor* and *City of Two Harbors.* Harry and Sam Goldish of Duluth owned the *Goldish* which they ran along the South Shore rescuing people from shipwrecks, in addition to the rest of their duties.

The *Grace J.,* operated by Christiansen and Sons Fishery, and the *Stanley, Richardson, Phelps* and *Siskiwit* were other names assumed to be part of that mystical fleet. The two-cylinder, hot-tube Kahlenberg engines were started on gasoline, then run with kerosene. They also used a sail for emergencies and for running through ice floes in winter, to save on propeller damage.

The biggest seasons were late fall and winter when frost smoke, storms and freezing weather obliterated their paths and iced down the dangerously overloaded hulls. There was no use for the Mosquito Fleet after roads were built around the lake. Trucks took over their job of hauling fish to market.

The demise of the boats was as mysterious as the beginning. The *Dagmar* ran aground and sank near Chippewa Harbor on Isle Royale while hauling beer to a Fourth of July party on Caribou Island. The *Elvina* was set adrift, disappearing below the waves outside of Two Harbors. The engine of the *Thor* was removed and sold to Martin Christiansen, then her plug was pulled and she was set adrift to her grave in Lake Superior. I'm sure some were pulled ashore where children played imaginary seafaring games that undoubtedly fell far short of the real adventures experienced by the rotting old hulks that smelled of fish and gasoline – and sometimes rutabagas.

The *Crescent* Trapped in Ice

Captain Johns of the Johns' Fish Company in Duluth took pride in the fact that his steamer *Crescent* serviced commercial fishermen along the North Shore and Isle Royale well into the winter – long after the other fish-carrying tugs had quit for the season. This service was well-appreciated by fishermen, and the company was rewarded with a large portion of the fish caught.

Traveling on Lake Superior in late fall was and still is dangerous. Extending the shipping season into December and January is asking for trouble. Extreme cold, strong winds and blizzard conditions are common and deadly, if caught on the lake.

Captain Johns' sons, Willie and Edgar, and a double crew of deck hands headed for Isle Royale in late December 1912 to bring supplies to and pick up fish from a few fishermen wintering over at Siskiwit Bay. Willie Johns was skipper, but it was Edgar Johns, the engineer, who narrated the story years later.

After being held at bay for a week on Wright's Island by a nor'easter that shoved a big field of heavy drift ice 10 feet deep into their path, the Johns and their crew headed for Pigeon Point on the border of Minnesota and Ontario. They loaded fish there and continued down the shore, stopping every few miles to load more kegs of salted herring and sacks of frozen fish.

By the time the *Crescent* got to Two Islands near Schroeder, she was grossly overloaded. The temperature was way below zero and ice forming around them on the lake eventually halted their progress. They were five miles outside Two Islands and frozen in by heavy ice.

The crew walked the five miles to shore, then proceeded 12 miles through the woods to a logging camp, where they made arrangements to have coal delivered to the icebound *Crescent* so they could keep the engine running and heat their quarters. They also sent to Duluth for ice saws. They spent the next month sawing a channel five miles to shore in order to get protection for the boat and crew behind Two Islands. If the ice pack shifted while the boat was locked in on the open lake, the boat would be crushed like a matchbox.

Half the crew deserted the ship to save their lives in what they perceived to be a deadly circumstance. The other half sawed the channel to shore.

Edgar: "We sawed our way in, and the ice was 36-inches thick. It was so darned cold out there that our sawcut would freeze up before we could go any distance. So I kept steam up and when they had sawed maybe 100 feet or so, I would jump aboard and open up the engine ahead and she would shove that great cake of ice down and away. Took us a month of very hard work, but we finally made it to shelter."

They wintered behind the islands, buying coal and groceries from the logging camp. In March, the lake ice finally broke up enough and drifted far enough from shore to allow them a quick dash to the safety of Two Harbors.

The tug *Torrent* came to their rescue by breaking a channel through the ice from the inner harbor to the lake channel, thus ending the *Crescent*'s nightmare of wintering on the lake trapped in a field of ice. The *Torrent* burned 80 tons of coal in the rescue.

Isle Royale Cowboy

Who was the Isle Royale Cowboy? In the book *Island Folk* by Peter Oikarinen, island resident and neighbor to the cowboy, Ingeborg Holte said that his name was Gilbert Leonard. But the last surviving member of the Leonard family says that the cowboy was none other than her father Erick Leonard. Gilbert was Erick's son, and it's possible he may have played cowboy on occasion, too. The exact year of the story is unclear, but all agree that it was sometime before World War I.

A few Isle Royale families kept a cow for milk and, if they wintered on the island, for meat. The animals were delivered by freight boat. Because the water was too shallow by the fishermen's docks for deep draft ships like the *America* to land, the cows were forced to "walk the plank," then tipped into the water to swim ashore to the fisherman's home.

According to Ingeborg, the Erick Leonard family lived on a small island in Malone Bay at Isle Royale where he was a commercial fisherman. Because the island was mostly trees and very little grass, the cow found grazing inadequate. But there were several other islands in close proximity to Leonard's with small areas of grass on each.

Erick solved the problem by rowing the cow to the islands to satisfy her needs. Each day he'd load the cow into the 18-foot, flat-bottom herring skiff and row the cow to greener pastures. Each night he'd pick her up and row her home. Ingeborg Holte said, "She stepped into the skiff and stepped out by herself. That's true, I saw it."

It wasn't long before the cow, growing impatient waiting for the boat ride, started swimming from island to island by herself. Said Ingeborg, "I was at Malone Island visiting the Malones when this cow came swimming over. At milking time she swam back to Leonard's again."

In researching the visual problems of the painting, I could find no eyewitness accounts of the way the cow stood, sat or laid in the skiff. Ingeborg and other witnesses are gone now, leaving no written record of whether the cow faced the oarsman or the stern of the boat. Relying on my imagination, I decided I'd rather look at the cow's face, no matter how close it was to mine. I also imagined, with that big face just inches away from the oarsman's, that there'd be some sort of social pressure to hold a conversation.

Several families "wintered over" on Isle Royale during hard times, choosing the hardships, loneliness and isolation on the island to the high cost of living on the mainland. They depended on cows, pigs, chickens, moose, fish and garden produce to get them through the long winter.

Hospitality in the Wilderness

I checked the engine down as my converted fish boat approached the dock at Pete and Laura Edisen's place near Middle Island Passage in Rock Harbor, Isle Royale. The door opened on the neatly painted house as Laura peered out, then stepped down the flower-lined path to the fish house, waving all the while to my family.

Pete stepped out of the fish house on the dock, still wearing his scale-spattered rubber pants. He grabbed my bowline as we landed. After hugs, handshakes and the usual greetings, we were urged up to the house for "coffee." In those days "coffee" meant a spread of smoked trout, pickled herring, cold cuts, cheese, fresh bread, pie and, of course, coffee.

Genuine hospitality was common along the North Shore and Isle Royale in the early days, when settlers led isolated lives that created a hunger for the company of other people. Friends and strangers alike were invited into warm homes, offered good "coffee" and entertained like royalty. Homemade music from the accordion, violin or piano was played for the guests, stories were told and questions were asked and answered. They wanted to know about their visitors and how things were going on the outside.

Pete Edisen was a natural storyteller. He entertained his guests with stories of shipwrecks, storms and his personal close calls on the big lake. Encounters with moose, beaver, wolves, caribou, otter, fox, rabbits and sea gulls were common, and all the animals except wolves seemed to feel at home with him. Only the wolves wouldn't eat from Pete's hand.

He'd also drag out his collection of semiprecious greenstones for visitors to admire – it was common for a guest to be given one as a gift.

Departing wasn't easy. They walked us to the dock, shook hands, gave tearful hugs and then stood waving a long goodbye. As we pulled away, Laura waved with a handkerchief – then a dish towel – finally her apron was all she had that would be visible as distance increased. (It reminds me of the old story: "How do you get a one-armed Norwegian down from a tree?" "You wave at him.")

Pete Edisen immigrated from Norway in 1916, started commercial fishing at Rock Harbor, met and married Mike Johnson's daughter, Laura. The National Park Service allowed them to continue commercial fishing on Isle Royale the remainder of their lives. Pete was 81 years old when he finally retired, after 60 years of fishing and hospitality on Isle Royale.

Justine Kerfoot of the Boundary Waters

The search for gold, silver, copper and iron ore gradually replaced the search for fur-bearing animals in the up-country between Grand Marais and the Canadian border. Henry Mayhew cut a road from Grand Marais to Rove Lake in the mid-1870s to service his fur trading post and to facilitate hauling out the silver ore he speculated to be in the Rove Lake area.

The Gunflint wagon road, built to serve the anticipated mining industry, became the Gunflint Trail that was finally extended to reach Saganaga Lake. The border lakes, known as the Voyageur Highway, were finally easily accessible to prospectors, miners, fur traders and sportsmen longing to hunt and fish the pristine wilderness.

Mining efforts failed, but logging and tourism still thrive along the Gunflint Trail. Woodsman/trapper Charlie Boostrom and wife, Petra, built the first lodge catering to sportsmen and tourists on Clearwater Lake in 1914. Lodges on Greenwood, Hungry Jack, Poplar, Seagull, Saganaga and Gunflint lakes soon followed. Most of the early lodges were Ma and Pa operations, with Ma doing the cooking, washing, cleaning and other chores, while Pa was off guiding the sportsmen guests. Women played a major role in the resort business throughout the area.

Justine Kerfoot is a prime example of one of the women in this wilderness. Justine's parents, the Spunners, bought the Gunflint Lake Fish Camp in 1927, seeking refuge from the Great Depression. Justine left college to join them, graduating with a major in zoology and a minor in chemistry and philosophy.

In her book *Woman of the Boundary Waters,* Justine says she learned the skills necessary to survive her new life from the Indian families living across the lake on the Canadian side. In short order, she became an expert canoeist, fishing and hunting guide, fur trapper, dog musher, carpenter, electrician, plumber and mechanic. She hired the cooking and cleaning help from her neighbors across the lake.

Justine married Bill Kerfoot and raised three children in that rugged wilderness setting, but she was the ramrod and driving force that eventually made the Gunflint Resort what it is today. Her son, Bruce, with wife, Sue, continues the family tradition.

Justine wasn't aware that she was a victim of male domination, and the feminist movement needn't take credit for her success. Justine accomplished what she did through grit, determination and love of the wilderness.

Pigeon Point to Grand Portage Freight Line

It was almost impossible to earn a living in 1929 during the Great Depression. Some men were forced to do almost anything, and many took great risks to put food on the table. Walker Matthews, who was raising his family in Grand Portage, heard of the plight of a small group of commercial fishermen on Pigeon Point. They had caught 2,000 pounds of herring just before the lake froze. The freight boats were unable to reach them to take the fish to market, which meant that the fish would spoil and the fishermen would lose the money necessary to make it through the winter.

To help his neighbors and make a precious dollar or two for himself, Walker rigged his sleigh, using only one bunk and one horse, and took off over the ice from Grand Portage across Wauswaugoning Bay, through the Susie Islands and then to Pigeon Point several miles away. A cold wind blew across Wauswaugoning Bay, driving the minus 30 degree temperature to the marrow of horse and man.

Walker and his horse, Dan, risked two trips that day along the frozen shoreline. Wind and waves had caused the ice pack to crack where the ice field was exposed to open water. Cracks and fissures opened and closed dangerously as the horse and sleigh crept along, fighting the freezing Arctic-like winds. By the time Walker and Dan reached the two-foot-wide channel of water separating the floating ice fields, Walker's hands and face were frozen and the horse refused to move across the open crack. If the wind shifted to the northwest, Walker, the rig and its precious load would drift out to sea on an ice floe that would eventually break into smaller pieces.

Knowing that they would both freeze to death soon if they didn't get to shelter, Walker unhitched Dan, freeing the horse to save himself without the burden of the heavy sleigh. Walker then trudged off to a fisherman's home on Hat Point, where he thawed out enough to walk to Grand Portage for help. He found Dan standing by the dock no worse for wear.

After warming himself by the stove and getting a bite to eat, Walker took Dan back over the ice to the sleigh and returned triumphantly to Grand Portage, where the truck was waiting to haul the fish to Duluth. The Pigeon Point to Grand Portage Freight Line was successful, even though it lasted for only one day. And that was fine with everyone concerned.

Teaching School in the Wilderness

Getting an education was difficult during the pioneer years on the North Shore and Isle Royale. Giving an education was even harder, as Dorothy Simonson's book *Diary of an Isle Royale School Teacher* documents for us.

Although Dorothy's diary is about her teaching experience during the winter of 1932-33, I'm sure it reflects similar experiences of teachers along the North Shore from the turn of the century, when that area, too, was isolated from the rest of the world.

Dorothy seemed eager to face the challenge of teaching Holgar Johnson's four children in Chippewa Harbor, even though it meant living in total isolation in very rustic conditions, with none of the services and conveniences she was accustomed to. She and her young son, Bob, arrived at Chippewa Harbor on the steamer *Winyah* on September 15, 1932.

"From where I'm sitting," she wrote, "I can look across 300 feet of clear turquoise water sparkling in the autumn sun, at a sheer rocky cliff, peopled with slim spires of evergreens. This is truly Isle Royale the Beautiful."

On the last trip of the season, the *Winyah* left the small group stranded with (hopefully) enough supplies to last the winter, plus a battery-powered shortwave radio and a malfunctioning wireless for communication with the mainland.

Dorothy started teaching with enthusiasm in the one-room schoolhouse, but her spirits gradually declined as winter wore on.

"Nov. 22 – For the first time we realized we are indeed isolated on this block of snow and ice, with its threatening fir-crowned cliffs and howling wolves, its frozen stars and frost moon, surrounded by nothing but a seething turbulence that men call Lake Superior."

Entries throughout the winter describe the terrible teaching conditions in the schoolhouse: "What a day – cold – the school is like a barn and all of us huddled around the stove, which simply gobbled wood.

"43 degrees below zero and a blizzard….Burned 30 huge logs… still cold….Bob wore six pairs of socks….I wore three…feet still cold."

Radio problems prevented contact with the mainland. Frozen batteries, provisions giving out, no vegetables, ringworm, hives, snow and more snow added to her discontent as winter worsened. By February and March, the marooned family longed desperately for the first trip of the *Winyah*.

"March 18 – The ice is piled up outside as far as we can see and hopes of an early boat are fast disappearing….

"April 5 – Oh Hell! Is all I can say. We're out of kerosene, so can't read, and almost out of butter, coffee and canned goods. I'm sick of moose meat and potatoes! The compressed yeast is gone and the other has soured….

"April 9 – No *Winyah*! We were really quite disappointed….I hope we hear her whistle tomorrow!

"April 14 – The gulls are screaming so today that I'm about to scream with them."

Then finally it happened:

"April 15 – Well the season's big day is over! The *Winyah* has been here!…When she whistled at the harbor entrance, I felt just like crying and was so nervous I just shook – felt much worse than the day she left! The *Winyah* needs a coat of paint badly – but she looked like the *Barengaria, Majestic* and the Vanderbilt yacht all rolled into one to us!"

Dorothy completed her teaching contract with the Johnson family and on May 2, 1933, she left for home with Bob on the *Winyah*. Besides the rough times, she also recorded many happy times during that winter. She reminisced frequently recalling that, despite the hard times, it was a rewarding time overall. She continued to promote the island until her death in 1984.

Art Sivertson's Automatic Washing Machine

I'm willing to share in the responsibility for my Dad's valiant attempt to create an automatic washing machine for my overburdened mother on Isle Royale. I'm sure my dirty diapers and wet bed clothes helped to create her burden, but doing the laundry for not only our family but for hired men helped to encourage the incident.

My father seldom got involved in "women's work." He was usually on the lake, fighting his own demons, trying to harvest fish from dawn to dusk. But once he happened to be working ashore and had the opportunity to witness the painfully hard work that Mother went through on washday. In sympathy, he helped her lug the water from the lake the 50 yards to the house. It took many trips to fill the copper boiler on the kerosene stove and the washtubs on the porch.

Dad anticipated the backbreaking work that followed as he counted many baskets of dirty laundry stacked on the porch. Then an idea hit him.

He instructed Mother to heat the water, but not to do anything else until he returned. On his first trip up from the fish house, he rolled a giant wooden barrel used for soaking nets in preservative. On his second trip, he wheelbarrowed the 10-horse outboard motor, with chicken wire fencing wrapped carefully around the lower unit.

After mounting the outboard on the inside of the wooden barrel, he put in soap, hot water and a basket of clothes. His eyes were brimming with excitement and pride as family members and hired men gathered to witness Dad's new invention at work. The moment was electric.

Dad gave the engine a crank, but hadn't noticed the throttle set on full speed. The screaming and pandemonium quieted only after Dad managed to find the spark plug and short it out to stop the engine. There were clothes and soap suds in the trees, on the roof and all around, as people stood frozen in fear and shock, staring at the abomination from whence came the eruption.

Needless to say, the result of the experiment did not warrant any further development or fine tuning. Not even a five-horse engine was considered as a possible alternative.

Dad turned his inventive genius to matters less frightening and more along the lines of his expertise. He created a knot used to firmly tie two pieces of seaming twine together that could be separated instantly with one hand and little effort. He understood a bit more about Mother's problems after that day, but Mom still didn't have the foggiest notion about what he went through each day on the lake.

Lake Ritchie Rodeo

Life was hard for the commercial fishermen of Isle Royale. The backbreaking work of harvesting fish required them to toil from before dawn until after dark, with few days off, for nine months a year.

They lived on an isolated island in the middle of Lake Superior, having little contact with the outside world. Some could enjoy a few minutes each day listening to the news and weather reports on battery-powered radios – when the reception was not too bad. Other than that, they created their own diversions to escape the monotony of work.

Milford Johnson was a commercial fisherman all his life on Isle Royale until he died while fishing at Amygdaloid Island in the early 1980s. When he was a young man, Milford took a few days off from fishing to guide Dr. Oastler and his wife on a sport fishing and photography trip to Lake Ritchie, southwest of Moskey Basin. The trip turned into an adventure, and Milford was fond of telling this story.

"I rode a moose one time. That was on Lake Ritchie. Doctor Oastler wanted to give me 50 dollars to do it. He kept on for several days. 'You're chicken. You're chicken. You're not going to do it.' So I got disgusted and said, 'Well, by golly, I'm going to try it.' So we paddled up to this bull moose. He must've been three or four years old. He wasn't full grown yet, but he was big enough. We got up right alongside of him, and I got on him from the canoe. He was swimming as fast as

he could, but we could easily catch him. And I hopped on him. So he headed for shore. I had to lie right flat on him, because he could get his hind legs up so doggone high he would've touched mine if I was riding him like a horse. I was worried. Lying on my stomach, I grabbed him by the antlers. And, boy, I was wondering how this was going to work out when he got on shore so that his feet could touch the bottom. I had to make sure that I got off before that happened. And I did. I was on him for about 10 minutes, and that was long enough. So I slid off, and was afraid of what was going to happen. I slid right back and gave him a little shove so he wouldn't touch me with those hind legs. By golly, that moose, he kept for shore. It wasn't far until he touched the bottom. Then he stopped. And, oh boy, I thought, now what's going to happen? That doggone Dr. Oastler was off quite a ways. He should've been closer. Now, I didn't feel so hot right then – for a minute or two.

"So I started swimming for the canoe, but the moose didn't follow. Then getting in the canoe was a job. Was that ever a circus! You can't get in over the side, but I finally got in over the end. I was a crazy, ragged thing. I thought I was going to rip my sock, but I got in. And then he was satisfied. He got his picture – and I got my 50 bucks."

– from *Island Folk* by Peter Oikarinen

H. Siverson
© 1995

"Gjem the Moose Meat! Hide the Gun!"

The game warden didn't suspect a thing as Grandma served him fishcakes, fresh bread, apple pie and coffee in the kitchen of her home on Isle Royale. Little did the game warden know that the kind, gentle woman humming old Norwegian hymns in the pantry was a lookout for the small band of moose poachers enjoying coffee and fellowship around the table with him.

The warden and the commercial fishermen were friends sharing the wild isolation of Isle Royale together as neighbors. He was especially active during the closed season for trout fishing, as he cruised the waters of the 45-mile-long island looking for illegal nets.

The fishermen stayed ashore for three weeks each October to allow the trout to come onto the reefs to spawn. Their supply boats ran fewer trips during this period, however, meaning the fishermen didn't receive fresh meat from the markets on the mainland as regularly as usual.

Moose were plentiful, to the point of overbrowsing and becoming a nuisance to the families living on the island during the 1920s and '30s. Mothers had to sometimes shoo the giant beasts out of their yards so children could go outdoors and play. The giant antlers of moose became tangled in clotheslines, strewing the fresh wash through the woods. In fly season, they scratched their massive bodies on the rough siding of the homes and stared curiously in the windows at the goings-on.

I often wondered as a child why it was considered manly for sportsmen to kill moose with a high-powered rifle, when any enraged, 100-pound mom could take one down with a baseball bat.

The fishermen of Isle Royale found it hard to respect Michigan game laws designed to protect the moose herd for "sportsmen," who killed the animals for their large antlered heads, while those who hunted out of a need for food were called poachers and outlaws. That kind of rationalizing came easy to the meat-hungry fishermen, as they witnessed the fat cows browsing along island trails. Usually, two moose were taken and shared with the Washington Harbor families each fall.

Grandmother's job was to watch for the game warden and sound the alarm: "Gjem the moose meat! Hide the gun!" she shouted at the top of her otherwise soft voice when she saw the patrol boat coming down the harbor. "Gjem" means "hide" in Norwegian and Grandma got Norwegian and English mixed together at times of excitement.

Quickly, the moose meat was buried under the sawdust in the ice house and the bones were buried under the woodpile. Dad sank the moose hide in the lake by loading it with rocks.

All was accomplished in jig-time, before the patrol boat touched the dock, where the warden was heartily welcomed. Once, while standing on the dock with the warden, Dad spotted the hide bob to the surface behind the warden's back. Apparently, it had belched out its load of rocks. Calmly, Dad suggested they all retire to the house for "coffee" and arrived at the table a few minutes after the others.

The game warden knew the fishermen took a moose or two each fall, and the fishermen knew he knew. He understood their plight, but was bound to do his duty, if evidence was left carelessly about – like a moose hide that inadvertently floats up under his nose.

Later, as the group stood on the dock waving goodbye to the warden, Dad noticed the moose hairs clinging to his wool pants and realized the pressure he'd put on his friend. The warden once again proved himself to be a gentleman.

Aakvik to the Rescue

Helmer Aakvik was a strong, rawboned man with hamlike fists and a lantern-shaped jaw. But his tough grizzled exterior belied his quiet intellect and soft-spoken sense of humor. He typified the hardy, robust characters who had the determination, independence and self-reliance to survive the hardships of pioneering days on Lake Superior's North Shore. Helmer was a herring choker who immigrated from Norway to fish herring and trout from his new home at Hovland.

On November 28, 1958, 63-year-old Helmer Aakvik defied death in an attempt to rescue his young friend and commercial fisherman Carl Hammer from Lake Superior's stormy and freezing waters. Twenty-six-year-old Carl had risked a strong northwest wind and below-freezing temperatures to tend to his herring nets the day before Thanksgiving. When the storm worsened and Carl didn't come home in time, Aakvik went looking for him, assuming that he had engine trouble.

Aakvik loaded his 16-foot skiff with an extra outboard motor and gasoline and pushed off into the frost smoke that obliterated his landmarks. He set his compass course to where he thought Hammer might have drifted in the strong offshore wind. The temperature dropped to 6 degrees, freezing the gas line of his 14-horsepower outboard. Seas were building to 20 feet as he drifted many miles from shore. He threw the useless motor overboard to lighten the hull. But it was too stormy to risk attaching his spare motor to the boat and try filling the gas tank while the boat was being thrown around in tumultuous seas.

In the morning, the wind subsided enough for Helmer to chance attaching his spare motor to the skiff. He filled it with all the spare gas he had and started in the direction of the shore. He came within one mile before running out of gas.

The Coast Guard found him "frozen to his oars and rescued him just in the nick of time." His skiff sank just moments later. Upon disembarking from the Coast Guard cutter at the dock in Hovland, Aakvik's only request was for a pinch of snoose. He remarked to his neighbors on the dock about the beautiful moon that night on the lake. When asked if he prayed for help in his time of peril, he answered in his heavy Norwegian accent, "No – there's some things a man has to do for himself."

Carl Hammer was never found. Aakvik survived his frostbitten feet and hands and continued his bout with the great lake, fishing commercially until he died in his early 90s.

The Uprising

The painting of Walter Caribou was inspired by the annual reenactment of the 1795 Fur Trade Rendezvous and Powwow Ceremony at Grand Portage. It is a reminder of the partnership between Indian providers and French and English fur traders that lasted for more than 200 years.

Ojibway Indians provided furs, food, canoes and guides to French, English and Scottish fur traders throughout western Canada and the United States. Without the Native Americans, there would have been no fur trade.

The Ojibway and French got along well, accepted each other's traditions, intermarried and raised families whose names still are common on the Grand Portage Reservation. Names like Drouillard, Deschampe, Duhaime, LeGarde, Cyrette and Gagnon are as common as original Ojibway names like Ashwains, Shingibis, Nabaub, Caribou, Spruce and May-Mush-Ka-Waush. Relatives of the Grand Portage Band extend over a large geographic area, crossing over state and international boundaries imposed by white politicians.

After the decline of the fur trade, Indians and Metis relatives carried on commercial fishing as independent operators or as employees of the American Fur Company at Grand Portage, North and South shores and Isle Royale. They helped harvest the white pine forests at the turn of the century. Men like Waub-Ojeeg earned fame as great leaders and warriors. Mokquabemmette (John Beargrease, father and son), are well-known as men who delivered the mail along the North Shore using rowboat and sled dogs from the mid- to late 1800s. John Beargrease Sr., Antoine Mashowah and John Morrison were Indian captains on the schooner *Charlie* during its heyday. Internationally known artist George Morrison is of Indian/Scottish descent with roots in Grand Portage.

Indians who chose a more traditional Ojibway life stayed on the reservation, or in the woods, on lakes and rivers nearby to hunt, fish, trap, harvest wild rice and make maple syrup. But the past 150 years were devastating for Native American cultures, as hordes of aggressive white Euro-Americans swarmed over their lands bringing alcohol, disease, unjust treaties and unkept promises that broke the spirit and eliminated the traditional lifestyles of the American Indians. There were Indian uprisings but, until now, all failed.

Today's uprising, happening in Indian communities all across America, has a good chance to succeed. It is an uprising in spirit caused by hope of a new economic base to provide dollars for reservation development. Proceeds from the Grand Portage Lodge and Casino, owned and operated by the Grand Portage Ojibway Band, are being reinvested in its community. The new community club is a wonderful example. An expanded marina, better housing, roads and overall living conditions are other examples of progress as the casino breathes new life into a grand community.

Who knows. With any luck, the Indians may finally use the white man's greed against him and win back some of their lands.

Isle Royale's Last Commercial Fisherman

Prehistoric and woodland natives harvested Lake Superior's fish to feed their families for thousands of years. The Hudson's Bay and North West Company voyageurs provided the fur traders with fish caught from the clear cold depths of Gitche Gumee during the 1700s and 1800s. Until the 1830s, the fish were used just for feeding members of the tribes and employees of the fur companies.

The American Fur Company became the first commercial fishery on Lake Superior, with stations around Isle Royale and the North and South shores. They harvested siskowet, trout, whitefish, sturgeon and herring for markets in the Midwest until 1842, when the company failed.

Indians and out-of-work miners continued to fish commercially on a marginal basis when they were joined by immigrant Scandinavian fishermen in the late 1800s. They brought new techniques from the old country and made commercial fishing a major industry on the lake for the next 100 years. They fished with gill nets, pond nets, seines and hooklines that provided consumers with low cost, nourishing, high protein food.

Commercial fishing provided food in the most efficient and economical way until the late 1950s, when several almost simultaneous things put an end to harvesting fish for food. A small voracious predator fish, the smelt, was introduced into the Great Lakes and reproduced rapidly by feeding on the spawn of other fish, including the lake trout. At the same time, sea lamprey arrived from the ocean through the newly opened St. Lawrence Seaway and promptly destroyed adult breeding-age trout. Within a few years, lake trout almost totally disappeared from Lake Superior from the impact of these two deadly predators.

Meantime, taconite tailings from processing plants on the North Shore were pumped into the lake and destroyed spawning beds and habitable water for herring and whitefish on the western end of the lake.

The takeover of Isle Royale by the National Park Service forced commercial fishing families from their traditional homes and fishing grounds through prohibitive regulations and attrition. Stanley Sivertson, a lifelong resident of Washington Harbor, was the last commercial fisherman on the Isle, ending a long history of harvesting fish for food. He fished almost to his dying day in September 1994.

The trout, whitefish and herring have made a strong comeback. Old-timers claim there are more fish currently in the lake than ever before in their memory. Government efforts to control the sea lamprey and discontinuation of taconite tailing discharge into the lake plus a program of restocking indigenous breeds have succeeded in repopulating the lake.

Even so, commercial fishing continues on the decline. Lake trout, which were once the major market fish for commercial fishing, are now classified as "game fish" and are reserved for the sport fishing industry. Except for Native Americans, who are allowed to harvest fish under treaty laws, and a handful of other commercial fishermen scattered about the lake, the business of catching fish for the market is about over.

Stanley Sivertson was the last commercial fisherman on Isle Royale. To me, he symbolizes the last of the hardy breed who harvested fish for food, not only on Isle Royale but on Lake Superior, the Great Lakes and some day the oceans.

The painting shows Stanley Sivertson and wife, Clara, baiting hooklines at Isle Royale in the 1940s. Commercial fishing was often a family operation at Isle Royale where wives and children helped out whenever they could.

The Last Woods Runner

As settlers pushed the American frontier west, an ever-increasing population encroached on and threatened the last vestiges of wilderness. Alarmed naturalists organized and had legislation passed that set aside a few areas preserving a wilderness state for future generations to enjoy. National parks, forest preserves and the Boundary Waters Canoe Area Wilderness (BWCAW) are examples of areas protected from our exploitation and destruction.

Restrictive regulations were imposed, limiting access in wilderness areas not only for recreational visitors but for the original inhabitants of the designated parks.

Resorts and individuals had to be bought out and forced to leave their homes and lifestyles to create the semblance of wilderness for weekend wilderness buffs. Some of those who had chosen to make the wilderness a way of life fought back with the belief that no one should be exiled from their lifelong homes and chosen way of life in America – especially to create a contrived wilderness for "city dudes looking for a wilderness experience."

Benny Ambrose from Otter Track Lake in the new BWCAW was one such citizen who fought back and won. Benny made his home in the Boundary Waters as a young man just back from fighting in World War I. He earned a living off the land, hunting, trapping, guiding and prospecting for minerals. He lived year-round in a canvas tent, where he and his wife raised two children. He finally built a log home on Otter Track Lake about 15 miles across water and portages from the end of the Gunflint Trail.

In 1948, the government started proceedings to buy out Benny, taking his life in the wilderness away from him in order to create the BWCAW Recreational Park.

Benny was to be exiled and his cabin burned to make way for the multitude of canoeists that would trample across his homesite, looking for a wilderness diversion from their hectic urban lives.

I'm not sure if it was Benny's threat that he had "a loaded 30-30 rifle in my cabin and will shoot the first government official who sets foot on my dock" that won his fight, or if the Forest Service had a genuine change of heart. But, he had already fought one war for his country and it would have been terrible publicity if he had to fight another for his rights against the same government he insured after his first fight.

Benny was given the title "Volunteer in the Park" and was allowed to live there until his death in 1982. A monument to Benny still exists on his homesite at Otter Track Lake.

The freedom to live in the wilderness that the Indians enjoyed for thousands of years and the voyageurs for 300 years is gone now. The *coureurs de bois* no longer hunt, trap or paddle canoes in the border lake country.

The last woods runner is gone.

Isle Royale Roy

'Here comes Roy!" was shouted by the first person to hear the engines or spot Roy's boat approaching any of the harbor homes on Isle Royale.

During his 50-year career, Roy Oberg operated five boats around Isle Royale, hauling mail and freight to the fishing families tucked away in the nooks and crannies of the island. But, no matter if he were aboard the *Woodshed, Rita Marie, Disturbance, Voyageur* or *Voyageur II,* the message was always the same – "Here comes Roy."

Like his grandfather, Axel Oberg, who immigrated from Sweden, and his father, Axel B., Roy was a commercial fisherman and a ship's captain. His father and grandfather built and operated the tugs *Elvina* and *Red Wing,* which were used to haul fish and freight along the North Shore and Isle Royale as part of the "Mosquito Fleet."

In 1936, Roy started running his own 26-foot boat, the *Woodshed,* to pick up fish on Isle Royale. In 1942, the newly formed Sivertson Brothers' Fishery hired Roy to skipper the 35-foot *Rita Marie* for the same mission. In 1945, the 38-foot twin screw *Disturbance* made three trips weekly from Grand Portage to circumnavigate the island with the additional duties of carrying mail and supplies. The 48-foot *Voyageur* replaced *Disturbance* in 1955. Roy retired in 1986 at the age of 75 from the company's newest and current mail, freight and passenger boat, the 63-foot *Voyageur II,* which started its run in 1972.

Hauling fish, mail and supplies were the income-generating services in the earliest days. Passengers were more a nuisance than a revenue source, and no attempt to accommodate them was considered. In later years, due to the decline in fishing and the increase in tourism, that situation was reversed.

Even though Roy entertained his passengers with colorful stories en route, it was apparent to some, especially after a particularly rough and stressful trip, that Roy preferred the old days, when the ice and dead fish didn't constantly ask questions and demand attention.

Many of Roy's 3,000 trips around Isle Royale were accomplished with limited navigational aids. His compass, watch and senses were all that this old salt needed as he smelled, listened and felt his way around the 200-island archipelago's reefs and intricate waterways. His absolutely perfect safety record in more than 50 years of navigating the most treacherous mail route in the world, in winds, fog, blizzards and every other kind of weather imaginable, is evidence of his acute senses and intimate knowledge of his route.

At each stop, Roy and his deck hand unloaded ice, gasoline, mail, empty fish boxes and miscellaneous supplies – including groceries and other store purchases for island residents. He'd take on boxes and kegs of fish, along with orders for more supplies and groceries. Some orders were written on scraps of paper, while others were shouted over the noisy confusion of loading and unloading. Roy remembered almost every verbal order, and no one was surprised when they got exactly what they had shouted for.

Even though Roy stopped piloting the *Voyageur II* in 1986, most of the old-timers still call out, "Here comes Roy," when they hear the whine of the twin diesels or spot the silvery ship approaching the harbor.

Roy passed away October 3, 1995, and I feel pretty sure some lookout at the Pearly Gates shouted over his shoulder as he saw Captain Roy ascending, "Here comes Roy!"

Epilogue

The drama continues on our North Country stage. The background scenery has changed very little, but the actors and plot have changed a lot. Isle Royale's Last Commercial Fisherman and the Last Woods Runner closed the curtain on the era of adventurous risk-takers, who set the stage for the next act of government, business and tourism in our modern era.

The natural resources of the North Shore and environs have been turned over to the recreation industry. The fisheries resource has been taken from commercial fishermen, who harvested fish for food, and given to sport fishermen, who catch fish for fun. The once proud lumberjacks are now criticized by environmentalists for providing the wood products to satisfy our own insatiable demands for paper and lumber. The forests are now regulated by the government for use by campers, hikers, canoeists and other outdoor enthusiasts. The resort and hospitality industry is growing, making tourism the star of our economic show, as fishing and lumbering exit stage left.

The wild, exciting frontier has left the scene. Our forefathers, who walked, sailed, canoed, skied, snowshoed and used dog teams for practical purposes involved with survival, have been replaced by offspring who walk, sail, canoe, ski and snowshoe for recreational adventures on weekends – the "been there, done it, what's next" generation.

The wild has been taken from wilderness by regulations, codes and rules that are designed to protect it from us and to, hopefully, preserve it for all time. The wild and woolly has been taken from the actors, too, through education and regulations that tend to inhibit our adventurous expressions.

The scenery backdrop to our northland stage remains essentially the same, except for a few obvious changes. The quaint fisherman's home, with fish houses, net reels, boats and slides that dotted the North Shore and Isle Royale, is gone now. Those on the North Shore have been replaced by modern homes of recent immigrants from the city, who tend to bring much of the city with them. New resorts and motels have changed the shoreline, but not enough to destroy its character. Yet. At Isle Royale, the colorful fishing family homes have been bulldozed and burned to recreate the Park Service's idea of wilderness. The logging camps with the muffled sounds of handsaws, wool-clad lumberjacks and heavy-breathing horses have been replaced by high tech machinery with roaring engines and rumbling trucks needed to harvest wood more efficiently.

But these are minor irritants in a wonderful country that still retains most of its original character. Lake Superior is still wild and beautiful, as are the Boundary Waters and Isle Royale. The sociability and hospitality of the folks who choose to live here are still second to none, reflecting their relatively stress-free existence in a place they've selected, above all others, to spend their lives.

I, too, love it here, but sometimes I miss the snoose-chewing kids who play with snoose-chewing moose. Where are the fishermen who row cows from island to island in wooden skiffs? I miss the snowshoe trails of trappers, the steam whistle of freight boats, the jingle of bells from dog teams bringing the mail, hobnailed lumberjack boots and fisherman's rubber boots covered with fish scales. I'd give almost anything to hear, once again, the sounds of fiddle, concertina and lusty voices singing the old Scandinavian songs that echoed among the islands.

Maybe I can keep some of those memories on stage with encores of more painted tales of the Old North Shore.

– Howard Sivertson

For Further Reading

Above and Below
by Thom Holden
1985 Isle Royale Natural History Assn.

The Diary of an Isle Royale Schoolteacher
by Dorothy Simonson
Isle Royale Natural History Association

History of Ojibway People
by William W. Warren
1984 Minnesota Historical Society Press

The Illustrated Voyageur
by Howard Sivertson
1994 Midwest Editions

Ingeborg's Isle Royale
by Ingeborg Holte
1984 Women's Times Publishing

Island Folk
by Peter Oikarinen
1979 Isle Royale Natural History Association

Julius F. Wollf Jr.'s Lake Superior Shipwrecks
by Dr. Julius F. Wolff Jr.
Thom Holden, contributing editor
1990 Lake Superior Port Cities Inc.

Lake Superior Indians
by Eastman Johnson and
    Patricia Johnston
1983 Johnston Publishing

The Long Ships Passing
by Walter Havighurst
1961 MacMillon

Once Upon An Isle
by Howard Sivertson
1992 Wisconsin Folk Museum

Pioneers in the Wilderness
by Willis H. Raff
1981 Cook County (Minnesota)
    Historical Society

Red Shadows in the Mist
by James Hull
1969 self-published

Ships of the Great Lakes
by James P. Barry
1973-1974 Howell North Books

Shipwrecks of Lake Superior
by James R. Marshall
1987 Lake Superior Port Cities Inc.

Shipwrecks of Isle Royale National Park
by Daniel Lenihan
1995 Lake Superior Port Cities Inc.

*The Superior Way: A Cruising Guide
    to Lake Superior*
by Bonnie Dahl
1992 Lake Superior Port Cities Inc.

Woman of the Boundary Waters
by Justine Kerfoot
1986 Women's Times Publishing

Other publications of Lake Superior Port Cities Inc.

Julius F. Wolff Jr.'s Lake Superior Shipwrecks
Hardcover: ISBN 0-942235-02-9
Softcover: ISBN 0-942235-01-0

Shipwrecks of Lake Superior by James R. Marshall
Softcover: ISBN 0-942235-00-2

Shipwreck of the Mesquite by Frederick Stonehouse
Softcover: ISBN 0-942235-10-x

The Superior Way, Second Edition by Bonnie Dahl
Spiralbound: ISBN 0-942235-14-2

Michigan Gold, Mining in the Upper Peninsula by Daniel Fountain
Softcover: ISBN 0-942235-15-0

Wreck Ashore, The United States Life-Saving Service on the Great Lakes
   by Frederick Stonehouse
Softcover: ISBN 0-942235-22-3

Shipwrecks of Isle Royale National Park by Daniel Lenihan
Softcover: ISBN 0-942235-18-5

Lake Superior Magazine (Bimonthly)
Lake Superior Travel Guide (Annual)
Lake Superior Wall Calendar (Annual)
Lake Superior Wall Map

For a catalog of the entire Lake Superior Port Cities collection of books
   and merchandise, write or call:

Lake Superior Port Cities Inc.
P.O. Box 16417
Duluth, Minnesota 55816-0417
USA
218-722-5002
888-BIG LAKE (244-5253)
FAX 218-722-4096